MERCY

FLASHPOINT BOOK 6

TARA ELLIS

MIKE KRAUS

MUONIC PRESS

MERCY
The Flashpoint Series
Book 6

By
Tara Ellis
Mike Kraus

* * *

www.facebook.com/taraellisauthor

* * *

www.MikeKrausBooks.com
hello@mikeKrausBooks.com
www.facebook.com/MikeKrausBooks

CONTENTS

WANT MORE AWESOME BOOKS?

Find more fantastic tales at books.to/readmorepa.

* * *

If you're new to reading Mike Kraus, consider visiting his website at MikeKrausBooks.com and signing up for his free newsletter. You'll receive several free books and a sample of his audiobooks, too, just for signing up, you can unsubscribe at any time and you will receive absolutely *no* spam.

* * *

You can also stay updated on Tara's books by following her Facebook page: www.facebook.com/taraellisauthor

SPECIAL THANKS

Special thanks to my awesome beta team, without whom this book wouldn't be nearly as great.

Thank you!

Twenty-two days. Less than a month since a cosmic event capable of destroying planets was aimed at the Earth. With only a glancing blow, the gamma-ray burst obliterated billions of lives in an instant. Unleashing a chain of cascading catastrophes, it brought the remaining population to its knees...and the brink of extinction.

With the ozone layer shredded, Earth's atmosphere has been transformed, its delicate balance of life-sustaining compounds permanently altered. The surface of the planet reaps the resulting fallout from the radiation, acid rain, changing weather patterns, and unusual animal behaviors. All electrical components were destroyed and communication made nearly impossible in the aftermath. In this new environment, it is imperative to adapt to the mounting obstacles just to survive, let alone flourish.

Danny. The fiercely independent woman was already on a journey of discovery when she found herself stranded over four hundred miles from her home. After pairing up with a chemistry teacher, Sam Ruiz, and a stray dog named Grace, she was forced to examine sides of herself she would have rather left hidden.

Throughout the unbelievable challenges faced along the way, her new friends and a young boy named Ethan emerged as Danny's lifelines. Against all odds, in the sea of confusion a rancher named Thomas Miller has become her anchor.

Tom. As a single father and owner of a large cattle ranch, he is the epitome of a good ol' country boy. Except nothing is ever as it seems, and Tom has his own demons to fight. He may have successfully delivered his son and friends to his hometown of Mercy, Montana, but it soon became apparent that their struggles weren't over. Finding himself thrust into a leadership role, Tom quickly learns that his sometimes-impulsive decisions have a broader impact now and might put everyone at risk.

Ethan. Ethan Miller is a lot like his father, and the teen has proven he's just as resilient. Being in Mercy and finding a new friend in Chloe has helped the healing process begin, so he can try and put the darkest days after the flashpoint behind him. While the constant challenges of everyday life offer a good distraction, there are other threats looming and he has yet to face his greatest hardship.

Chloe. Though she might have started out her journey as a troubled teen on a trek for redemption, Chloe Benson has been one of the few to keep a level head when so many others fell apart. Incredibly intelligent and intuitive, she's aligned herself with people who appeared to understand what it would take to survive. Now, together with Ethan and his family, she will fight alongside them to protect Miller Ranch and the place she has come to call home.

Patty. As a retired nurse and the mayor of Mercy for several years, she did all she could to keep her town from falling apart after the gamma-ray burst. Having stepped down as mayor, she plans to focus on healing instead of leading. Fate might have something else in mind. With the danger from the military, outlaws, and others unseen approaching, her role may not be that easy to define.

General Montgomery has never questioned his role or his destiny and he still believes it is up to him to save those left alive in the United States. He's so sure of his tactics that he'll do anything necessary to stop those who oppose him, including the leaders left in the civilian government.

Master Sergeant James Campbell, leader of the Marines Special Operations Forces, 1st Force Reconnaissance, was one of the weapons in the general's arsenal. James might be a loyal soldier, but he's also a patriot. When his orders required him to turn on the civilian government, he took matters into his own hands. James and his team have marshaled a US senator into hiding, and he's about to be reunited with his father. While he suspects they're all a part of a greater scheme, the endgame is more complex than he could have imagined.

Russell Boyd's plan is just getting started. He has many places to go and countless lives to end in order to rid the Earth of its infestation. The flashpoint was the greatest thing to have ever happened to him, and only proved that he'd been on the right path all along. A path filled with righteousness and synchronicity. Russell may never be done, but he'll happily play his role until he's no longer needed. First, he has work to finish in Mercy.

All have been led to the small mountain town of Mercy, Montana for different reasons. In this final episode, their lives will collide as they fight for love, justice, power, and their very existence.

CHAPTER 1

RIC
Location Unknown

THE DARKNESS WAS ABSOLUTE. Like a blanket, it covered Eric, smothering him as if it were something tangible. Clawing and pulling, it threatened to drag him down into the deepest recesses of his mind.

A light flared, erupting into the space and transforming some of the blackness into dancing shadows. Eric flinched, cowering from the shifting forms and whimpering as he desperately tried to ignite a pile of wood.

Eric.

He froze at the whispered word, his fear overriding his need to see and allowing the lighter to go cold in his shaking hand. Blind again, he jerked back to attention and fumbled with the device, his thumb sliding off the striker four times before it caught. His rapid breaths sounded like a sick, gasping dog and he swallowed once and licked his lips, forcing himself to slow his breathing.

Eric.

"No, no, no," he pled, his voice small. His lips stuck together as he mouthed other words that wouldn't quite form, all the while holding the small flame to first one stick and then another. Finally, one took and he focused on it, kneeling in close and blowing just enough to give the fire life.

We're here, Eric.

"Go away!" Eric was on his feet and screaming before he could control his movements. One of his feet knocked a log aside, scattering some of the wood. Sparks rose, winking out of existence as they drifted in front of his face. "Just like all the people," he moaned, while looking around, dazed.

Enough of the kindling kept burning so that he remained in a limited patch of illumination, but everything beyond the fire's small perimeter remained hidden. Eric couldn't remember where he was. He raised his hands and splayed his fingers along his forehead and face, pressing against his skull until it caused pain. When that didn't work, he slapped himself once, hard.

They're all dead, Eric.

"Shut up!"

Eric turned in a circle, disoriented. Was he in a cave? No. A basement. He was in the basement of someone's house. Not his.

The floor was suddenly beneath him, his face pressing into the cold cement. Memories came rushing back of the light in the sky, the darkness and confusion in the days following. He and Myra had gone to the mountains. To their cabin.

"M…Myra," he stuttered, sucking up dirt from the floor and crunching it between his teeth. "Myra!" Pushing himself up onto his forearms, Eric strained to see into the corners of the room. Was Myra there? Is that who was talking to him?

Shame suddenly welled up in his chest, a familiar feeling he'd wrestled with for over a decade, ever since his diagnosis.

The clozapine. Eric shut his eyes, trying desperately to hold on to the clear thought. To follow it back to something more coherent like a trail of breadcrumbs. He'd run out of his medication over a week before. He'd been okay for a couple of days, and then it started. The voices. The paranoia. Hallucinations and an inability to think or speak comprehensibly. Normally, he was a properly functioning, intelligent man of thirty-six. He'd maintained a steady job and relationship for years, against the odds, thanks to the medication. Without it, the schizophrenia crawled back into his brain and slowly took over. It...

It's coming for you, Eric.

He was back on his feet. Something was in his right hand. Something cold, hard, and heavy. The room was dark again.

The Bic was already in his other hand and Eric successfully lit it the first time. He was still in the basement, but the fire had gone out. How long had it been since his last lucid moment? His thumb began to burn as he dropped to his knees and he ignored the pain as he held the flame against what was left of the kindling. It must have been dry because it caught immediately, and he watched as the orange tendrils curled around the sticks, caressing it while devouring it, much like...

You have to stop them, Eric.

Movement.

Eric leapt to his feet and brought the object in his right hand up, hefting the rifle into place as he swiveled to face whatever was down in the basement with him. He could smell it now; a wet, dank, rotten odor. It reminded him of the time he dug up their pet cat several days after its death, because he wouldn't believe it was dead. He was twelve, and had recently watched *Pet Sematary*, which filled his head with wild notions that had been harder for him to discern from reality than other kids.

There was nothing there. No oily form slinking in the corners, waiting to lure him close enough to drag him down to hell. Perhaps he was already there.

"No…no. I'm alive. I'm here. I don't know where here is, but I'm somewhere. I'm nowhere. I…" Eric's muttered words trailed off as a pressure exploded in his head, causing him to gasp. He staggered back several steps before whirling around, pointing the weapon at any unforeseen demons at his back.

They're here.

Sounds from above. Eric shook his head, trying to rid himself of the pain left behind like a lingering shadow. That was how he'd come to describe the random attacks that were often the prelude to a bad…episode.

Thump…thump…scrape.

There was someone there. In the house with him. *They* were coming to get him.

Eric began to sob, his thoughts spiraling towards the black pit he knew he wouldn't come back from. Not without help. Not without the medicine. Only, there wasn't any more medicine. There wasn't any—

Don't let them take you, Eric. ERIC…ERIC…ERIC…

"N—no, no one. I—I—can't…won't take me." Eric shuffled forward until his feet hit the base of the stairs. His eyes reflected the flickering firelight as he squatted, wide-eyed, with the rifle pointed in front of him. Rocking slightly, someone close by might have mistaken the low sounds he made as humming, instead of the incoherent ramblings of a madman.

"Eric?" Myra called timidly. "Are you down there?"

A small sliver of natural light crept down the stairs as the old, wooden door creaked open a few inches.

Eric froze. Was that Myra? No, she was gone. They were all gone. He was already dead and this—

They've come to take you.

A red mist began to engulf the light on the stairs. It pulsed like it had a heartbeat, a sulfuric smell spilling ahead of it as it grew larger…closer.

"I won't go!" Eric wailed.

The sun was just beginning to rise over the small glen, where the rustic cabin sat amid a cluster of pine trees. A stream meandered through the clearing, alive with fish and life-sustaining water. It would have been an ideal spot to ride out the end of the world. To start over.

A shot cracked through the stillness, causing birds to take flight. A minute later, a second round rang out, and then the valley fell into a deep, eternal silence.

CHAPTER 2

DANNY
Miller Ranch, Mercy, Montana

MIST ROSE FROM THE FIELDS, chasing away the last of the night as a howling wind turned it into writhing tendrils of ghostly apparitions. The air was heavy with pent-up energy on the verge of being released, and birds took flight in advance of it.

Danny stared up at the angry, churning clouds and cursed under her breath. It was horrible timing. Her feet were already damp from the dense morning dew that clung to the overgrown grass surrounding the farmhouse, and her sweatshirt wasn't enough to keep out the chill. Her hair smelled like woodsmoke from the morning fire and her hands were already dirty.

While they'd managed to get a decent amount of the field cut the day before, there was still at least two days of work left to do. Danny could only guess how the hay would be affected by being bundled and stacked wet. Sandy was nearly frantic about it, waking everyone before dawn to get started on their tasks.

Danny was dismayed to see that it looked like the rain could let loose at any minute.

She was quickly coming to understand how much juggling of priorities were involved with running the farm, especially under the current circumstances. Sandy had taken Sam with her at daybreak to go check on how the calving was going, while Ethan went to ride the line of the upper field in advance of the storm. He was concerned that he might have missed something since he hadn't checked it for a couple of days. Having hay wouldn't do them any good if the cows weren't alive to eat it. Danny was impressed with the teen's work ethic and it was obvious that he took his dad's request to watch over things very seriously.

She had also taken Tom's last-minute request to heart, and had already gone through the room above the barn. Danny was initially confused when she saw the radio, but after sifting through the papers left on the desk, it was fairly apparent what it was all about. That didn't explain whose radio it was or why Tom asked her to look into it, but the logical assumption was that it belonged to Bishop. That would also explain why he wanted her to look through his personal belongings.

"Come on, Grace," she called absently. The retriever was uncharacteristically antsy, pacing back and forth and occasionally whining. Danny figured she picked up on everyone's nerves as they waited for word about the ambush, in addition to the looming storm.

She unclipped the radio from her belt and tried to reach someone for the third time that morning.

"Miller Ranch to Mercy Base. Over."

Danny frowned at the radio as nothing but static was returned. She knew it would probably be several more hours before Tom and the others were close enough to reach anyone. Even with the repeater boosting the signal, they had to be within a certain number of miles from the guard at the south end of town. They would then relay it on. However, the ranch could normally communicate with anyone in Mercy, and sometimes even the guard station, thanks to the enhancement of the signal. When they were greeted with static that morning, Sam suggested that the storm was likely running interference, which made sense, but it still ratcheted Danny's anxiety up another notch.

A gust of wind blew her hair forward and across her face as she walked toward the barn, and Danny pushed it back impatiently. She was frustrated as well as irritated about not knowing what was happening to Tom, or with the storm and isolation. And because it felt like she was violating Sandy's trust by sneaking around her farm and going through her friend's things.

Danny almost let Sam in on her secret mission, wanting to seek out his advice, and even went out to the bunkhouse the night before after discovering the radio. However, as soon as she stepped into the room, he'd immediately begun to go on about his indoor farming plans. He was so excited that Danny couldn't bring herself to drag him down into yet another problem. She was determined to handle it on her own.

Glancing back over her shoulder, Danny confirmed that Chloe and Crissy weren't behind her. They were supposed to be headed for the hayfield to start cutting. They would have a nice stack ready for her by the time she got a couple of horses saddled and prepared to haul the bales to the barn. The six of them had worked out a good system during the long hours of work the previous day. Although sore, Danny was actually looking forward to the hard labor. It helped clear her head and gave her a stronger sense of purpose, both things she was actively trying to improve on.

A horse neighed and stomped in response to a larger gust of wind as Danny rounded the corner of the barn. Instead of entering, she continued to the bunkhouse and paused at the door. She knew Tom wouldn't have asked her to spy on Bishop if it weren't important. Given the discovery of a secret radio…she guessed the implications could be far-reaching. Gathering a breath, she pushed through the entrance and blinked a few times as her eyes adjusted to the gloomy interior.

Sam might be rather brilliant, but he was a horrible housekeeper. His bed was unmade, with clothes strewn across it. A towel and mismatched dirty socks were piled next to it on the floor. Four cups, all half-full of liquid, were sitting on the only table, along with several sheets of paper and two notebooks. Randomly stacked wood had fallen to the side of the woodstove and scattered across the floor so that Danny nearly tripped over it.

Bishop's half of the room, on the other hand, was tidy and well kept. His bed was even made with sharp corners folded in the covers and his bag was neatly placed at the foot of it, on the floor.

Already feeling guilty, Danny grabbed the large hiking backpack and set it on the bed. Unclasping the top, she gingerly reached in and took a few items out one at time. A comb, bug spray, and deodorant. She wondered why Bishop hadn't taken it with him, and figured it was because such a large bag would be cumbersome on a horse, and unnecessary for such a short trip. Sighing, Danny fully committed and, lifting the bag, shook all of its contents out onto the bed.

Two changes of hiking clothes and a pair of extra shoes fell out. There were also several pairs of socks, a useless flashlight, and a first-aid kit. She felt like it was getting harder to breathe as Danny heard a noise and looked up to find Grace sitting in the middle of the room, watching her. "Don't look at me like that," she muttered, turning her attention back to the bag. She was taking too long and needed to get to the horses.

There were several side pockets and the inside one contained the first item of any interest. It was an old photograph of a younger Bishop and teenage boy, although they were close to the same size. Danny could see the resemblance and assumed it was most likely his son. Hadn't someone said he had one that was supposed to be in Germany when the gamma-ray hit? There was nothing written on the back, so she set it aside. The only other thing in the pocket was a compass. Except it wasn't an ordinary compass, but an ornate piece made from silver and inside there was an engraved message:

Colonel Campbell

May you always find your way home

Campbell? Danny didn't know what Bishop's real name was, so the compass could belong to anyone...but she was certain it was his. She found it very believable that the man served some time in the military, and although that might give her reason to doubt him, the effect was just the opposite. If nothing else, Bishop seemed like a man of integrity, and the one thing Danny was still sure of was her gut. It had never let her down.

She hurriedly started to place the contents back in the bag, trying to remember how they'd been packed. Giving up quickly, Danny huffed and randomly jammed it all inside. It would be better if she confessed, anyway. He'd probably understand.

The door swung on its hinges, moaning as another gust of wind blew into the room. Danny jumped at the sound and dropped the backpack to the floor as Grace whined again. The dog smacked her chops and jumped to her feet, ready to leave.

"Okay, Grace, I'm with you. Let's get out of here." Relieved that she didn't find anything incriminating, Danny ran for the stalls, eager to get the horses saddled and underway for the day. She grabbed at the radio as she went, trying one more time.

"Miller Ranch to anyone on this channel. Can you read me? Over."

Random clicks and more static. Danny was pretty sure that meant someone was at least trying to talk to her. Whether or not they could hear what she was saying, though, she had no way of knowing. "If you can hear me, I'm unable to read you. Please update with any information on the group if it comes in."

Gritting her teeth to keep from cussing again, Danny went to re-clip the radio, but paused when she caught movement out of the corner of her eye. She was in front of the large double doors of the barn, looking to the southwest. The girls should be southeast of that location, and everyone else was nowhere near there. It was essentially the back part of the main property that adjoined all of the various trails and roads into the eastern fields.

Grace began to growl low in her throat as Danny froze and searched for the source of the motion. She knew she wasn't imagining it—Grace's reaction only confirmed it.

She was being watched. Although she couldn't see anyone, Danny knew instinctively that she wasn't alone. Slowly, she reached behind her for the edge of the door, getting ready to dive inside.

Before she'd even touched the wooden frame, a loud shot cracked nearby and Danny's head simultaneously whipped around as something struck it. She could still hear the sound echoing as the ground rushed towards her and everything went black.

CHAPTER 3

HLOE
Miller Ranch, Mercy, Montana

"I HAVE to go see him tonight! I don't care if it's dark out," Crissy insisted. Dropping the armload of tools she was carrying, she turned to Chloe and stuck her hands on her hips. "Trevor is going to think I've forgotten about him!"

Snorting, Chloe reached for one of the sickles, the blisters on the palm of her hand reminding her to put her gloves on. "I don't think that's possible. Besides, you missed one day, Crissy. One. Day." The insane wind churned the dirt at their feet, sending a billowing cloud of dust up and around them before dissipating. It was going to be an interesting day.

Chloe wiped at her stinging eyes and stood with the sickle before pulling at her gloves, then stopped and bit her lip to keep from scoffing again when she saw the look on her friend's face. The girl was serious. Unbelievable. "Look," she said instead, trying with every fiber of her being to not make fun of Crissy.

"We're getting such an early start out here, I'm sure we'll manage to have dinner at a decent time. I'll offer to go with you, so Sandy shouldn't protest, even if it's dark out."

Crissy beamed. "Really, Chlo?"

Feeling a little guilty, she nodded eagerly. "You bet!"

In reality, Chloe was only offering because she knew Ethan, being the gentleman that he was, would insist on going with them. The two of them could then duck out of the clinic after visiting with Trevor for a few minutes and attempt to have some fun. Patty had said she was welcome to sort through the supplies in the basement of City Hall. She could use some soap, and even though it would be kinda late, Chloe was hoping to catch Caleb there. She really wanted to show Ethan the transcripts from the mystery transmissions and get his take on it.

Thinking about Ethan prompted Chloe to pause and look out across what was left of the hayfield. She knew he'd be gone for at least a couple of hours, and that it was important to make sure the cows were secure, but he definitely made the time pass more quickly when he was with her. Ethan could also cut an impressive amount of hay in a short span of time. The sooner they finished with the grueling chore, the faster they could move on to everything else. Like implementing her plan for digging out the water trough and getting to work on Henry's Hollow. He still needed to show the cave to her.

"Have you asked Ethan to the dance yet?" Crissy asked, moving up next to Chloe.

She looked over at her friend, assuming she was joking. "You can't be serious."

Crissy positioned her hands on her sickle so she had a good grip before taking a practice swing. "Why wouldn't I be?" She wrinkled her nose at Chloe. "Life must go on."

"You *do* know what's happening beyond this farm, right?" Chloe demanded, her voice holding more contempt than she'd meant. Crissy looked at her with a pained expression. Of course she knew. Her friend wasn't stupid; Crissy was just good at ignoring the upsetting stuff and focusing on the mundane. A characteristic Chloe had never embodied. She took a slow breath and tried again. "Don't be surprised if they cancel the dance, after all that's happened the past few days. But we'll still have the barbeque," she rushed to add, determined to be positive about something. "Everyone has to eat, no matter how messed up things get."

Chloe took several brisk steps until she reached the end of the row, and had a clear view up the hill. She faced into the wind, squinting, and was surprised that she didn't see Danny headed their way. Looking for her would be a good distraction, because she couldn't handle the conversation anymore. She'd gotten better at walking away from confrontations, instead of being so…Chloe-like. "I'm going to check on Danny," she called back to Crissy. "She's taking too long. Maybe she needs some help!" Her words were torn away by the wind, even though they were less than twenty feet apart. Crissy waved absently in acknowledgement and began swinging at the base of the tall grass.

It was early morning, though it was much darker than it should have been, thanks to the gathering clouds. Chloe glanced up nervously at the lightning that was beginning to flicker through the base of the storm. Each time another bolt hit, the experience was worse than the last, and that was saying a lot. She'd never been afraid of storms before, but that was partly because they were predictable to a certain degree, and she knew what to expect. An odd strobing of bluish light preceded a hollow-sounding reverberation reminiscent of an alien vessel descending from the sky, punctuating Chloe's thoughts. "Sometimes I wish I didn't have such a vivid imagination," she scoffed, quickening her pace until she was almost running.

Nearing the top of the hill, her legs were already burning and she slowed, noticing at the same time a strange sort of ozone smell. It was similar to the scent after an intense rain, or right before... Chloe froze, looking at the tool she was still holding. The long metallic blade on the end of the pole would be perfect for attracting electricity. Tossing the tool aside, she turned towards the barn that she could finally see in the distance. What in the world was Danny doing up there?

Chloe spotted Grace first, as the dog ran back and forth. Frowning, she began to walk faster again. Something was definitely up. Danny was poised at the entrance to the barn and before Chloe could call out to her, there was the unmistakable sound of a gunshot.

Ducking out of instinct, Chloe continued to rush forward and watched in horror as Danny flew backwards and fell to the ground. Another shot, closer than the first, and the ground near her feet erupted as a chunk of earth was scooped out.

Someone was shooting at her.

Gasping in shock, Chloe threw herself behind a tractor that was already beginning to rust. A bullet ricocheted off it as her face met the ground and she scrambled forward on her hands and knees. She could see Danny's feet just inside the barn. They were moving.

Closing her eyes in an effort to hold back the tears, Chloe took a deep, shuddering breath. "Get a grip, Chlo," she muttered. She could hear Grace whimpering, and it spurred her into action. Eyes flashing open, Chloe gauged the distance from the edge of the oversized farm equipment to the barn door. It wasn't far. Getting her feet under her, she crept ahead and readied herself.

"One...two..." as she whispered *three*, Chloe launched herself at the opening. She landed hard on her hands and knees next to Danny, as another bullet harmlessly hit the side of the building.

There was so much blood that at first that was all Chloe could focus on. "Oh, God," she muttered, reaching for Danny. "Please… please be okay."

Moaning, Danny had both of her hands on her head, partially covering her face. Blood oozed between the fingers of her right hand, and it had pooled in the dirt under her. She lifted her right hand in response to Chloe's words and waved her off while struggling to sit up. "Rifles," she was whispering. "Get the rifles, Chloe."

Chloe blinked, and rocked back on her heels. Danny was talking. She was talking, so that meant she wasn't going to die, right? Wait. The rifles. She was right. Someone was *shooting* at them, and they needed to shoot back.

Staggering to her feet, Chloe looked around the gloomy barn, her thoughts hazy. The rifles should be by the door. The doors! Spinning back, she sidestepped the opening. Leaning into one half of the sliding doors, she pushed against it with all of her strength. The heavy structure shuddered in its tracks before sliding into place, effectively hiding them both.

Taking several slow, measured breaths, Chloe's head began to clear and she moved with more purpose. There were two rifles stored on the wall in a gun rack near the main entrance. She went to it, lifting down first one and then the other Winchester. They were both loaded and there was a box of .30-30 ammunition sitting on the top of the rack. She grabbed the box and then turned back to Danny.

Grace was all over her, licking at her hands and trying desperately to get into Danny's lap. "I'm okay, Grace," she said weakly. Wrapping her right arm around the dog's shoulders, she pulled the retriever close and stared up at Chloe. "I think it's just my ear."

Chloe found that hard to believe, but wasn't about to insist that Danny remove her hand from the wound. She was conscious and talking so that was good enough for the moment. "Did you see who it was?"

Danny coughed once and then closed her eyes briefly before giving her head a small shake. When she spoke again, her words were clearer. "No, but whoever shot me wasn't the same person I saw, so there's at least two of them."

Chloe nodded in agreement. "Yeah, two different people were shooting."

"There are probably more." Danny tried to stand, disrupting Grace from her lap. She made it as far as her knees and then stopped, blinking furiously as more blood dripped from where her hand was clasped. She struggled out of her sweatshirt and balled it up against her head to staunch the flow.

Chloe rushed to help her, but Danny waived her off again and sat back down. "Give me one of the rifles, then go and see if you can spot anyone. Here," she added, reaching awkwardly for the radio at her waist. "See if you can get through."

After giving Danny a rifle, she cautiously peered around the door she'd pulled across, being careful to avoid the rest of the open space. Without exposing herself, she couldn't really see much. Frustrated, she tried the radio. "Hello. This is Chloe at the Miller Ranch. Someone is shooting at us. Can anyone hear me?" After a few seconds of silence, there were several clicks and only static. "Great."

"Here," Danny was reaching for her, so Chloe went and gave the radio back to her. "Go and look out the other end," she instructed, pointing at Chloe. "But be careful. It's got to be the desperados. They must have used the Miner's Trail."

Chloe didn't think she could feel any worse, but the suggestion that they were being attacked by a group of homicidal outlaws ratcheted up the fear factor. "Crissy!" she gasped, horrified she'd left her friend alone. And what would happen when Sandy, Sam, and Ethan walked into the attack unknowingly? Motivated by the need to protect her friends, Chloe ran to the other side of the barn, and its regular-sized door. It was already standing partway open, so she sidled carefully into the space and peered out.

She could see part of the hayfield from there, though Crissy was at the lower end and out of view. Thankfully, Chloe didn't spot anyone else there, but there were two riders on horseback between it and the barn. They were rough, dangerous-looking men, both armed with rifles. One was poised almost directly in front of Chloe, between her and the farmhouse, while the other was to her right, in the direction of the Miner's Trail and upper fields. A third man, on foot, walked between them and it looked like he held a pistol.

They were being surrounded.

Anger suddenly surged and mixed with Chloe's fear, and the extra adrenaline rush nearly took her breath away. If the men managed to surround them, and there were as many outlaws as Tom suspected, she and Danny were dead. Or worse.

Chloe moved without hesitation, not allowing herself time to think through her actions. Otherwise, she might chicken out. Dropping to a knee, she engaged the lever-action and then brought the butt of the rifle snug against her shoulder, just like Bishop had taught her.

The man on horseback was less than fifty feet away and a perfect target. She thought of Danny, bleeding on the ground behind her and what the men would do if they got inside the barn. Chloe pulled the trigger.

CHAPTER 4

ANOTHER SHOT. There was no question anymore that they came from the ranch.

Tom's chest tightened more at each report, until it was difficult to draw a breath. They were too late. The outlaws were attacking his family and it was his fault they were left unprotected.

"Tom! We can't keep up," Bishop shouted as the rest of the riders fell farther behind him. "And your horse is about to drop."

Lilly's steps faltered and she barely caught herself before pressing on. She was frothing at the mouth, sides heaving. Tom knew Bishop was right. The mare would drop dead before stopping. He'd been pushing her beyond any rational limits the whole night, only resting a handful of times. They were so close.

"Whoa," Tom called to her as he straightened in the saddle. "It's okay, Lilly. Take it easy, now." He studied the road ahead as she slowed to a trot, estimating they had another three miles to go. He could run on foot the rest of the way if he had to, even though he wasn't much better off than the horse.

Tom had been awake for nearly thirty hours and operating off sheer determination for most of the night. When they were unable to raise anyone on the radio as they neared Mercy, their concern worsened. It could have been from the approaching storm, but it seemed unlikely…and calculated. If the military was involved in some sort of plot to take over the town, destroying the repeater would have been a smart move.

The week before, it had taken Tom's group a little over a day to travel from the outlaw's camp to the ranch. However, they were at the tail end of a long trip and also stopped when it got dark. He knew that if the desperados were motivated enough, it was possible they'd reach the farm first. In spite of that, Tom hadn't lost hope until the first shots echoed through the valley.

They'd just reached town and were barreling down Main Street. Although it was early, there were plenty of people around and they were able to recruit a couple of them, including Chief Martinez and the deputy left on duty.

The fire chief galloped up next to Tom, his horse fresh and full of energy. "You can take my mount," he offered. "We'll be close behind you."

Lilly reluctantly came to a stop at Tom's insistence, and he had no doubt the horse knew something important was happening. She snorted at him and tossed her head as he dismounted. "It's just for a couple miles," he promised her while resting a hand briefly on her nose.

"Bishop told us it was the military who sent these guys on the trail to your farm," Fire Chief Martinez said, scowling. "Now they're using criminals to do their dirty work?"

Tom hesitated with his foot in a stirrup of Martinez's horse. He'd had a lot of time to think about all the different scenarios during the long hours of the night. None of it made much sense and was a disturbing turn of events. "Dillinger is a calculated man," Tom explained, swinging up onto the gelding's back. "So I don't see this as a desperate move, or because he didn't have enough of his own men."

He pulled the horse's head around to aim him back up the street as Bishop and the other riders caught up. Tom wasn't about to sit around and chat, so he spurred the horse into action before finishing the conversation. He'd already come to the conclusion that the ordered raid was likely a means to an end that involved less risk for Dillinger if it wasn't successful.

Tom's anger flared again and fresh rage made his head pound. The corporal wanted Mercy and this was a way to weaken them, but it was more than that. Dillinger also wanted revenge for what happened at the FEMA camp and Tom was his target. It was personal.

Another shot jerked him from his thoughts and Tom was about to find out how fast the horse could go when someone ran out into the road from the trees to the west.

"Help!" Chloe screamed, holding her arm up and waving it frantically at the approaching riders. Her other hand was weighed down by a rifle.

Tom's breath caught when he recognized the girl, and the first thing he noticed was the blood on her hands and face. "Chloe!" he shouted back, reining his horse in only feet away from her.

"They're there," she gulped, sucking in air and trying desperately to form more words. "The outlaws. At…the farm."

"We know," Bishop said as he jumped down next to her. Carefully, he took the weapon and put an arm around her shoulders. Tom recognized that she was in shock, but they didn't have time to be gentle with her.

"How many are there?" Tom demanded, ignoring the look

Bishop gave him. "How did you get away, and whose blood is that?"

"Tom!" Bishop said, his voice rising. "One question at a time, or she isn't going to be able to tell us anything." Handing the rifle off to Sheriff Waters, he took Chloe by the shoulders and leaned forward to look her in the eyes. "Take a breath, Chloe. You're safe now. We need to know what's going on up there so we can help."

"I shot someone," she said, her eyes widening. Chloe glanced over at the sheriff, as if worried he'd arrest her. "I think I might have killed him."

"You did what you had to," Bishop reassured her.

Tom glanced anxiously back up the road, unsettled by the lack of gunfire. It could mean that there wasn't anyone left to shoot at. They needed to keep moving.

"I did!" Chloe replied, refocusing on Bishop. "I had to. They shot Danny and were surrounding the barn. I tried to stop them."

Tom's throat tightened and he barely restrained himself from getting off the horse and shaking the girl for more answers. "Danny's been shot? Where's Ethan and Mom?"

"Her ear," Chloe muttered, staring blankly at Tom and sounding dazed again. "She said it was just her ear, but it was bleeding *so* much. I saw Ethan and Sam," she rushed to add, like she suddenly remembered something important. "They came up behind the other guys and started shooting at them, so they backed off. That was when I ran. Danny made me. She said I had to go for help. You need to help them. Hurry!"

"Give her Lilly," Tom barked at Martinez. "Go to Patty's, Chloe. You'll be safe there. Tell Patty and Caleb what's happening."

Tom didn't wait for confirmation that his orders were being followed. Reaching out to where Lilly stood, he yanked his rifle from the scabbard as his horse reacted to his kick and leapt forward. A half-mile from where their long, private drive veered into the woods, he pulled up and headed for an unmarked trail. Looking back, he saw that Bishop and Waters were on his heels and was reassured by their shared expression. They were two men he wanted by his side when heading into battle, and he knew they were committed to protecting the same people he loved.

The implications behind the attack extended far beyond the ranch. If they didn't stop them here, it would be seen as a sign of weakness, and the town of Mercy would be even more vulnerable.

They had to make a stand, and it was his responsibility as both the owner of the ranch and now the mayor to send a strong message to Dillinger. Miller Ranch wouldn't be overrun like Duke's, and the town of Mercy was not going to become his next refugee camp.

Tree branches slapped at Tom's face and his hat was blown off his head as the storm seemed to let out one final, furious breath before unleashing the rain. Amidst a crashing volley of thunder and the sudden curtain of rain, three more rapid shots underscored it all, causing Tom to smile. He knew he must have looked maniacal as he crashed through the woods, weapon raised, but he didn't care. The gunfire meant there was still a fight to be won, and they were about to join it.

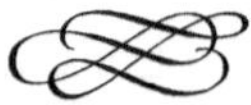

CHAPTER 5

AMES

> *Master Sergeant, US Marines, 1ˢᵗ Force Recon-naissance*

Trek Thru Trouble Office, Central Montana

JAY DROPPED his pack onto the floor of the waiting area in the Trek Thru Trouble office, and scowled at James. "This doesn't smell right."

James withheld comment on his friend's observation and instead kicked at his gear. "Just make sure the team's ready to move in a half-hour. We'll be rendezvousing with the helo and pushing our luck on how far she'll take us."

Gunnery Sergeant Jay Terrell smacked his lips before standing at attention. "Yes, sir, Sarge." As James turned to go, his friend grabbed ahold of his arm to stop him. "At least find out what's going on here. Because we both know it's not all about redeeming lost souls."

Senator Jenson walked in through the front door and paused when she saw the two men. "Is there a problem?"

She was good at reading people, James acknowledged. He had to give her that. "No, Senator," he lied. "Just finalizing our plans. We'll be underway in thirty minutes."

"I'm not sure how I feel about leaving Nathan here," she said, studying James. "I'd rather keep him with us."

James tried to maintain a neutral expression, but it was hard for him not to react. The woman might have a knack for picking up on things, though he kept having to explain simple logistics to her. "Hawk's injury will heal, but if he comes with us now, he'll slow us down and become a liability." When the senator continued to stare at him without comment, James proceeded with what he thought was only obvious. "The helo is already on fumes, so we'll be lucky to make it halfway to Mercy. That means we'll be walking for upwards of two days, which Hawk is clearly unable to do. That's why he has to stay here."

"I understand all of that," Senator Jenson said slowly. Why she was irritated with him, James hadn't a clue. "I thought soldiers had a code of honor about never leaving a man behind. I don't feel right abandoning him here."

James rolled his eyes and huffed once, no longer caring about hurting her feelings. "We aren't in the middle of a battle and he's not being deserted. I'm not about to bring those two kids with us and we can't leave them here alone. We need Hicks, so Hawk *offered* to stay here. It's safe, Senator, and it's better for everyone."

"Oh." Senator Jenson crossed her arms over her chest and frowned. "Well, why didn't Lucas just tell me that in the first place?"

Now it all made sense. "Sergeant O'Grady isn't known for being the best at communicating." James glared at Lucas as he stepped in behind the senator and gave them all an innocent look.

"What'd I do now?" he asked.

James turned his back on the ensuing conversation between the two men, which was sure to be full of insults and crude jokes. He almost felt bad for leaving the senator with them. Almost.

Leaving the front lobby, he traveled down a short hall with a couple of offices opening off of it, and into a larger, central room. It was set up like a locker room, with bench seating and rows of cabinets for storing gear. The door on the opposite side led to a kitchen and communal eating area, and beyond *that* were a couple of dorm rooms. It was an impressive setup. According to the rushed tour Hicks gave them the night before, it was designed to house all of the guides throughout the summer. It also served as a layover point for the kids before they left on their hikes, which sometimes lasted for several days.

James could care less about the hiking company. He needed to know what his father was involved in, and he was done playing games with the captain. Or rather, Hicks, as he was intent on calling himself.

They'd spent the night on rotating shifts to patrol the area between the building and the helo to watch for any movement. James had spent the first half of the evening staring into the dark woods. Then he crashed for a few hours in the dorm, knowing he wouldn't be any good without some sleep. Hicks had obviously gone out of his way to avoid him since daybreak and James was about to call the man out in front of everyone. He was getting to the point where he wasn't worried about whether information was top secret or not. They'd moved well beyond that formality.

James stomped loudly through the dorms. Ignoring the two teen boys sitting on their bunks, he opened the door into the counselors' sleeping quarters without knocking. Hicks looked up as he entered and didn't seem surprised. James slammed the door behind him.

The captain pointed at the door and scowled. "The theatrics

really aren't necessary, Sergeant. I know you have questions. I was hoping to make contact with your father this morning so I could get clearance to—"

"Screw clearance!" James shouted, taking another step into the room. "I know you've been holed up in here for a while, *Hicks*, so I'll cut you some slack. But it's time for a reality check. My whole unit is AWOL after disobeying orders from a Four-star General who is currently in charge of what remains of our country. I've got a kidnapped US Senator in my possession, and I need *your* help to locate my father, who somehow has ties to a geneticist and this place," James spat, lifting his arms and gesturing to the room around him. "Now, are you going to tell me what it is, or do I have to tear this place apart? Because I will, starting with you."

Hicks came out from behind the desk he'd been standing at and leaned casually against the front, crossing his arms. His demeanor was calm, but James recognized the look in his eyes, the way he positioned his hips, and how he placed his feet. He might have appeared relaxed to a casual observer, but James knew he was ready to react if necessary. The man had guts. Before he could test his true grit, he noticed a radio sat on the desk, and the comment Hicks made sunk in. "Wait a minute. You've been in contact with my dad?"

Hicks smiled. "Finally, a sign of intelligence."

"Can we skip the normal insults and posturing to find out whose is bigger, and cut to the chase?" James demanded.

"I've been making regular contact with him for a week." The captain leaned over and grabbed at some papers. "We determined it was best for me to stay here at The Farm, and for him to stay hidden in Mercy. While he made it onto the military's radar, our cover here doesn't appear to be blown. The identities we use at Trek Thru Trouble are buried as deep as possible, with no way to make a connection. He never should have told you about it."

"It's a good thing he did," James retorted. "And how are you getting your current information?" James asked, his confusion only deepening.

"I got the ham radio operating a couple of days after the gamma-ray burst," Hicks explained. "One nice thing about the radio was that at least during the initial confusion I was able to garner some valuable information without having to identify myself. I have multiple contacts within the military," he offered, without further explanation.

"You call this place The Farm?"

"It'll make sense soon," Hicks said. Opening a drawer, he took out what looked like a digital keycard.

"You said you haven't had contact with my dad in two days." James watched as the other man moved to a second door he hadn't paid any attention to. Opening it, Hicks looked back and gestured for him to follow.

"That's right. He failed to make our prearranged check-ins and I've been scanning hourly since the first miss. I caught some chatter from Malmstrom, though, and it sounds like there might be a move coming soon against Mercy."

James followed him into what looked like an anteroom of a containment facility. It was only about ten square feet and had a bench with hooks above it on which lab coats hung. "What sort of move?"

Hicks shrugged. "Unknown. It's hard to get much detail with Q-code when you're scanning and the reception already sucks. Except you know as well as I do that any coordinated military action involving a community is bad news right now, in our current state." He held the card up to a scanner secured to the wall on the side of the door and James was surprised when he heard a beep and a green light flashed above them.

"You've got power?"

Hicks looked back at him with a crooked smile. "The Farm

does."

James leaned back and took ahold of the outer door, pushing it back and forth slightly. It was much heavier than it should have been. He stooped and examined the door frame, then rapped his knuckles against the inner walls. "Metal. This is EMP hardened?"

"Among other things." Hicks reached beyond the door and a light turned on, illuminating a flight of stairs. He began the descent and then stopped on the fourth step to see if James was following. "You coming? If you want answers, you'll find them down here."

"My last few experiences with secret underground bunkers haven't gone all that great," James replied, following anyway.

It was a deep stairwell, with two turns and platforms before ending at another anteroom similar to the one over forty feet above them. The space was too small for his liking. James grew more agitated when Hicks stopped in front of the next doorway and stepped aside without opening it.

"Come on," he urged, trying hard not to sound anxious. "I thought you didn't like theatrics."

Hicks smiled again and pointed to a strange-looking contraption on the wall. The captain was enjoying the odd tour way too much. "Breathe into that."

"What?" James stared at the square metallic device. It had something resembling a circular speaker with a two-inch diameter on the front of it, and that was all.

"There's a very short list of people who have access to The Farm, Sergeant," Hicks said. "Breathe into it if you want to see what's inside."

Feeling silly, James bent over and blew onto the speaker. For a couple of seconds, nothing happened. Then, there was a deep, mechanical rumbling and the door slowly slid back into the wall. Long banks of fluorescent lights began to wink to life beyond the entrance as James looked over at Hicks. He frowned. "That BS traffic stop outside the base a few months ago that ended in a breathalyzer?"

Hicks shrugged again. "I had nothing to do with it."

"I knew that felt like a setup," James muttered as he stepped into what could best be described as an endless chamber of filing cabinets. Fancy filing cabinets. The room was so vast that he couldn't tell how far it extended in any direction. It was massive. "I don't get it. What is all of this?"

"A seed vault," Hicks said without any preamble. "A very advanced, state-of-the-art, never-before-created seed vault."

James wandered about twenty feet inside the vault and stared at his surroundings, utterly confused. If he'd been forced to make a list of all the potential types of covert projects he thought his dad was involved in, he would have never, *never* suggested a seed vault. "I don't get it."

"I don't expect you to," Hicks said without any surprise or contempt. "I'll make this very simple. Have you ever heard of the doomsday vault?"

James turned around to face Hicks. "I think so. It's in another country, though. Right?"

Hicks nodded. "Yes, and it's nothing compared to what we've got down here." When James continued to stare blankly at him, he continued. "About five years ago your father was approached and made part of a very small, select design team. It involved Dr. Pamela Watson because she is a leading plant and animal geneticist. This vault," Hicks said with enthusiasm while waving a hand, "is so much more than seed storage. It represents mankind's greatest chance of surviving the years to come."

James tried to focus on the implications behind what was being divulged and found he was having a hard time, considering the scope of everything else that had and was still unfolding. Genetically modified seeds and animals. "Modified for what?"

"To withstand an unstable environment." Hicks turned back

to the door, the tour apparently over. "Essentially, what we'll be facing once the atmosphere has settled into its new norm. Different pH levels, less water, altered temperatures."

"And the general knows about this place and is willing to lie and kill people to find it?" James wasn't convinced.

Hicks took a deep breath as he stood in the doorway. "Yes. Because he knows that even if he manages to regain control of the people, none of it will matter if he can't feed them a year from now. We're talking about *extinction*," the captain implored, his voice rising. "There are three of these vaults, and whoever ends up controlling them will wield more power than anyone else throughout history. The power to decide who lives and dies, and how it will all happen."

The impact of the truth behind those words hit James hard enough to steal his breath. He gasped once before he could swallow, and tried to regain his composure. It always came down to power. Hicks was right that at the dawn of their new existence, it was all going to be reduced to land, food, and the ability to grow it.

"We need to go." Hicks was no longer smiling and he had a new, nervous energy about him. "I was hoping your dad would have checked in this morning and my concern proved unfounded. I'm afraid we made a mistake not leaving last night."

"The bird can get us farther in a half-hour of flight than we could have walked all night in the dark," James countered. "And I hope your contacts are still good, because I've got a message for you to send before we leave." He shoved past the captain and began up the stairs two steps at a time, feeling a new sense of urgency. The underlying feeling of a continuing synchronicity compelled him to act without giving it as much thought as he normally would. In that moment, all that mattered was that they needed to find his dad before anyone else did. They had to get to Mercy.

CHAPTER 6

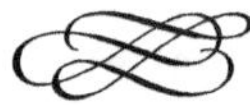

ETHAN

Miller Ranch, Mercy, Montana

"I LOST HIM!" Ethan muttered frantically as he scrambled forward on his stomach to the next tree, struggling to see the far side of the barn. He had joined the fight late and was still trying to get into a good position so he could help Sam and Sandy.

He'd heard the first gunshots when he was over a mile up the fence line. By the time he was within view of the scene playing out, Chloe was running away toward the road, with only the barn in between her and ten armed men. Calling them men was an exaggeration. They reminded Ethan of Decker and Billy, with the same lack of concern for hygiene and an air of disregard for life…and sanity.

Some of them were laughing. *Laughing* while taking potshots at the barn, where he assumed Danny was returning fire in a vain attempt to keep them away. Sam and Sandy were located directly west of the barn, and it was only because of them that the outlaws hadn't advanced any further.

It had to be the outlaws, because who else would be attacking them? Ethan questioned a lot of things as he watched two men on foot less than thirty feet below him attempt to sneak through the trees. Were they after the cattle? If so, there were ways they could have done it without any confrontation. That led him to believe they were either in a rush, or wanted the fight. Maybe it was both.

Sandy finally noticed the two creeping her way and put a slug into a trunk right next to one of their heads. Ethan couldn't help but smile as he watched them scatter. That guy probably needed a change of shorts.

A snapping branch behind him replaced the smile with a startled gasp and Ethan flipped onto his back to see yet another man successfully getting past him. Pressing his lips into a thin line, he chastised himself for not paying more attention, and allowing himself to get distracted. If Ethan let the guy go, he'd work his way up behind Sam and Sandy and the two would be caught in a crossfire. Danny would be left on her own, and the other guy he'd already lost sight of was probably on the far side of the barn by then. They were outnumbered and about to lose their only advantage. He couldn't let that happen.

Up until that point, Ethan had managed to land a few accurately placed shots to effectively deter the desperados. He knew the gunfire would be heard throughout the valley and that help would be coming whether Chloe reached anyone or not. He'd been hoping they could hold them off until support arrived, except their best gunmen were all on a wild goose chase.

Ethan grimaced at the irony as he pushed himself cautiously up onto his knees, never taking his eyes off his prey. The guy looked to be in his late twenties, though it was hard to tell for sure; he was so dirty. He was holding a pistol of some sort and was fervently licking his lips due to either nerves or excitement.

The Winchester was unnaturally heavy in his hands and Ethan willed his arms to stay steady as he stood and aimed the weapon. "You're gonna want to stop right there and drop that gun." His voice was surprisingly even and had the desired effect.

Freezing, the man's tongue remained sticking out as he slowly pivoted to face Ethan. Then, his eyes widened and his upper lip curled into a hideous snarl. He looked more like a rabid dog than anything human, and he began making a noise that was a cross between a wheeze and a grunt. Ethan realized he was laughing.

"Big mistake, kid," he sneered.

The lip, the way he called him kid, the *smell* of his rank body, all reminded Ethan of Decker. When he saw the man's forearm flex in preparation to fire, he didn't hesitate to pull the trigger first.

They were close enough that it would have been nearly impossible for Ethan to miss. And he didn't. The outlaw flew back with a grunt, the gun falling harmlessly from his hand to land in the soft pine needles. Ethan stood staring at it for a moment, confused.

The woods around him receded, to be replaced with first the nightmarish scene of bodies and burning tires in downtown Pocatello when Billy killed all those people, and then on the road North of Virginia, Idaho. It was when he'd watched Decker die. Ethan experienced the same, hollowed out feeling he'd had that day as his hearing returned and the trees came back into focus.

He was still staring at the gun, and Ethan shifted his view to take in the feet of the man he'd surely killed. They weren't moving. *He* wasn't moving. Another volley of shots forced him back to reality and he took a ragged breath, his lungs feeling as if they were being squeezed.

Bark erupted from the tree trunk near his head as a bullet

ripped into it, and Ethan flinched when the splinters stung his cheek and forehead. Instinct took over, saving his life, as he dropped to his stomach and barely avoided a second shot close behind the first.

There were too many of them. Pulling the Winchester out from under his body, Ethan tried to find something to aim at, but the foliage was too dense. Instead, he fired randomly into the sky, hoping it would at least give his attackers something to think about. If he could just buy some more time—

Shouts came from the direction of the road. A literal *war cry*, followed by the sounds of several horses stomping into the back pasture amid a fresh round of firepower.

"Tom!" Grandma Miller screamed, her voice full of both terror and pride.

Dad?

Ethan dared to poke his head high enough to take in the scene playing out below where he was concealed. Sure enough, more than a dozen new riders filled the space around the barn and farmhouse. It was obvious they were eager to fight, as they were all armed and already shooting.

Bishop was off his horse and taking a knee. Ethan watched as he gunned down a man approaching the doors of the barn, and then seamlessly pivoted to shoot a second who was running at him.

Horrified but also enthralled, Ethan knew he had to help and was in the best position to prevent anyone from circling around on them, or getting away on the Miner's Trail. Feeling somewhat numb, he fought through the weakness in his legs to make his way down the treed hillside, hoping Tango would remain where he'd secured him to a fencepost. The gelding would be spooked by the shots and could break free if he tried hard enough.

Ethan emerged at the far end of the field behind the barn. The same one they'd ridden into only a week ago, to be reunited with his grandma. A man lay moaning, begging for help, but he ignored him. Ethan could tell by the clothing that it was one of the outlaws, and he wasn't going to stop and risk anything for him. Not then, although he figured the man's wails would find their way into a fresh round of nightmares.

The storm had let up momentarily but was once again hammering them with rain and wind, making the farm look like a surreal battlefield from the Middle Ages. Men screamed, a woman shouted, followed by another shot and more screams. Ethan's nose tickled with the acrid smell of gunpowder as it mixed unnaturally with the fresh, earthy smell of a rainstorm.

Wiping at his face, he struggled to make sense of what he was seeing. It was more difficult through the downpour to tell who was who, although most of the outlaws were on foot. There couldn't be that many left. He knew at least six of the ten were down, and probably more by then.

A blur of movement from near the hayfield drew his attention, and Ethan swung his rifle up to track a lone man running toward him. It wasn't anyone he recognized, though it was hard to be sure. Hail mixed in with the rain and lightning strobed around him. As it became obvious the guy was heading for the trail, Ethan aimed low. Steeling himself, he took the shot and watched as the runner tumbled, hard, before writhing on the ground, grasping his leg.

"Ethan!"

His head snapped around, and Ethan saw his dad running toward him. He was holding a rifle, his head was bare and wet, and he'd never looked more dangerous. "I'm okay!" Ethan called out as he brought a hand to his face and wiped away the blood oozing from where the splintered wood had pierced his skin. The rain would wash away the rest.

Tom slowed, his shoulders relaxing slightly as he closed the rest of the distance. "Thank God you're okay," he said, taking ahold of Ethan's arm and giving it a squeeze. "I was afraid I'd lost you all."

"Chloe and Danny?" Ethan asked, concerned by his dad's comment.

"Chloe's fine," Tom said, glancing back over his shoulder and carefully surveying the edge of the field while he spoke, his dripping hair whipped around by the wind. "Danny's shot, but I think she'll be okay."

"I'm sorry," Ethan said, unsure why he felt a need to apologize. "I was up checking the line when they got here. I should have—"

"I'm glad you weren't here," Tom said, cutting him off. His hand suddenly tightened on Ethan's arm and pulled him backward, almost off his feet.

Ethan saw him then, another man making a break from the trees, trying desperately to flee to the trail. When his dad didn't react, he began to lift his Winchester.

"No," Tom said, putting his other hand on the rifle and pushing it down. "It's okay. Let him run all the way back and tell Dillinger how he failed."

The storm abruptly retreated again, offering a disturbingly clear view of the battle zone. Ethan looked around at the bodies, the injured, and several people—friends, who were walking towards them, blood evident on several of them. He met his dad's gaze and raised an eyebrow questioningly. "*Did* he fail?"

CHAPTER 7

ATTY

Mercy Clinic, Mercy, Montana

To say that their resources were overwhelmed would have been a gross understatement.

Patty paused in her task to push back some stray hair, using the edge of her gloved hand since the fingers were covered in blood. She'd hoped to never see the clinic so full of patients again, especially not all at once. The injuries ranged from a twisted ankle suffered while jumping off a horse, to a horrendous gunshot to the stomach. That man had finally succumbed to the wound after screaming for three hours straight even though Melissa gave him some morphine.

Fortunately, the only fatality was one of the outlaws. By some miracle, Mercy hadn't lost any of their own. Although they had suffered multiple casualties.

"The last of the…um, bodies have been stored in the garage," Sheriff Waters said as he approached her and Tom. She wasn't certain if he was giving the update to her or the new mayor, and she supposed it didn't really matter.

Tom nodded in response, not taking his eyes off of Danny, who was currently having part of her ear stitched back on to her head by Dr. Olsen. "How many in total?" he asked.

"Eight," Bishop answered. He glanced first at Patty and then over at the sheriff. "Eight dead, and that includes the guy who died here."

"Where are the other two?" Tom demanded; his voice gruff. "We need to talk to them. Now."

"One of them is sedated," Melissa said, looking up briefly to take another threaded needle from Patty. "He might not make it without some advanced care and possible surgery. The other guy's fine. The one Ethan intentionally clipped in the leg." She paused then and narrowed her eyes at Bishop. "Was it really necessary to *kill* so many of them?"

Patty flinched at the look Tom directed toward the doctor, and was thankful he had enough control to not respond. Instead, Danny was the one who reached up and grasped Melissa's wrist. "I know it must look like a bloodbath," she whispered, clearly in a lot of pain. "But we were the ones who were attacked. They didn't leave us much choice."

"I know. I'm sorry," Melissa sighed, closing her eyes. "I'm just so tired of death."

"We all are," Tom said stoically. "That doesn't make it go away, and I'm afraid this is only the beginning. We're going to have to be ready to fight for our town if we want to keep it."

Sandy was on the next bed over, and she sat up then, staring at her son. "What does that mean, Tom?"

Patty eyed the bandage wrapped around Sandy's upper left arm, and noticed it was bleeding through. She really needed stitches, but the stubborn woman insisted the bullet graze was just a "scratch" and refused care other than the dressing and a sling.

Bishop sat down next to her and put an arm around her good shoulder. "While we obviously didn't find the outlaws waiting for us at the road, we did find a messenger."

"What sort of messenger?" Sam asked. He was hovering at the foot of Danny's bed with Grace. The retriever was a quivering, whimpering mess and had been since Patty first saw her come into the clinic. She was such a sweet dog, and Patty sincerely hoped the trauma Grace experienced wouldn't leave a permanent mark.

"Dillinger was behind this," Tom said bluntly.

Danny gasped and started to turn her head in response. Thankfully, Melissa had quick reflexes, and jerked the needle back in time. "Danny, you have to stay still!" the doctor scolded, scowling at Tom. "Maybe you guys can wait to have this conversation until later?"

"No," Danny insisted. "I won't move. We've already wasted too much time this afternoon, if the military is involved. We need to know what's going on. Everyone does."

"We can call for a meeting," Patty suggested. "I don't think it'll be possible to do it tonight, but we can arrange to get everyone together first thing in the morning."

"Good idea," Sheriff Waters agreed. "Meanwhile, I've already added four more guards to either end of town, and two scouts to patrol several miles both north and south."

"Caleb went to check the repeater," Bishop added. "The storm passed over an hour ago and the radios still aren't working at any distance. I suspect it was taken out intentionally."

"Because?" Sam led, looking for further explanation.

"That kid from Bishop's hiking group who caused trouble at the farm before," Tom said, looking at Sam. "We caught him carrying a response to Dillinger, accepting orders to take the cattle."

"They've already taken over the Duke Ranch," Bishop added.

Patty looked at the man she'd come to trust with her life over the past few weeks. Something about him had changed. He'd always seemed to be holding back, and now it was like his whole personality was out on the table and she wasn't sure she liked it. It was like he was detached and more methodical. Sure, he was showing some concern and affection toward Sandy, but everything about him was…colder. More sterile. "How do you know that?" she asked, closely gauging his reaction.

"That doesn't matter right now," Tom interrupted, puzzling Patty even further.

"What does matter is that we're clearly next on the agenda," Bishop said. "Why he would use those outlaws instead of his men is still a puzzle—"

"Because they don't have any rules," Ethan spoke over him as he walked up. "I got a chance to know the corporal and I guarantee you he probably didn't have orders to do this, so he found another way. His men will come in through the front door while his dogs do the dirty work."

Patty was shocked by Ethan's words. Not only because it sounded accurate, but that the teen would be astute enough to put it together in the midst of what was going on. His face, which had finally been almost clear of bruises, was once again marred. Several deep scratches and puncture wounds peppered his right check and forehead and his eye was already swelling.

"He's right," Tom agreed. "Dillinger isn't going to stop."

"How are we going to keep the military out of Mercy?" Sam asked, kneeling down to comfort Grace. "We saw what they did in Monida."

"We'll discuss our options tomorrow at the meeting," Tom

said, looking at Patty. "You're right. The town leaders and council need to be a part of this discussion, as well as the solution."

Patty smiled at Tom in a silent acknowledgement, relieved he grasped the bigger picture. It wouldn't matter if a group of them decided to take action if the town wasn't behind them. Avoiding an invasion would require everyone in Mercy if they were to have any hope at all.

"There," Melissa announced, applying a final dressing to Danny's head. "I'm afraid your ear is going to be disfigured. It didn't seem to be affecting your hearing, so I think it should heal up pretty good. Of course, I don't have any way of scanning your head, so we can't be sure the bullet didn't crack your skull. There's no obvious fractures or chips that I saw before sewing it up."

"Um, okay…too much information," Sam balked, looking pale. He released Grace and she was immediately in Danny's lap before she'd even had a chance to position herself properly in the bed.

"Thanks, Melissa," Danny said while fending off kisses from Grace. "I'm not too concerned about my future modeling potential."

Patty was impressed, again, with the woman's resilience. Danny was most definitely a fighter and she was glad to have her in Mercy. Though it was too bad she'd been injured. They could really use her help patching up the rest of their patients, which reminded Patty that she hadn't seen Russell anywhere. She assumed the priest would have come immediately and offered assistance upon hearing of the attack.

"Chloe," she called out when she saw the teen approaching. "Do me a favor and go find Father Rogers. He should be at the church. Tell him I sent for him. We really need him here." Chloe glanced over at Ethan, her face falling.

"I'll go with you," Ethan volunteered. "I'm not much good here, anyway."

Chloe smiled and Patty was relieved to see it. She'd been worried about her since the girl arrived on her doorstep, bloody and traumatized. Patty knew she was in shock and it had taken over an hour before Chloe could even stop shaking. Being around all the chaos in the clinic really wasn't the best place for her, so the errand would accomplish two things.

"I'll meet you back here, Dad," Ethan said to Tom before the two walked away.

"Let's go talk with the leg-guy," Bishop said, standing. "Maybe he has some information that'll give us a better idea of when to expect more company."

"He might not be that talkative," Patty said, glancing at Melissa.

Melissa sighed again, a clear sign of how tired she was. "You all know how low my medical supplies are right now. When I was trying to treat the two…desperados, or whatever you're calling them, I had several people object to my using any medication on them."

"Seems reasonable," Sheriff Waters said, shrugging. "Why waste it?"

"Well, being humane aside, they might be able to tell you more if they're alive and not in unbearable pain," Patty snapped. She could tell that the sheriff and probably Bishop were going to try and argue with her, but Tom shut them down.

"Give the guy some morphine, Melissa," he instructed, while holding a hand up to placate the other men. "Unless you guys wanna buy him a few drinks, it's probably the quickest way to get him talking."

Patty chuckled as she backed away, leaving the group to debate the finer points of interrogation. She had to admit to being disheartened earlier in the day. First, it was the news of the attack, then the fact that Tom had led the march in the wrong direction, and finally the lack of humanity in deciding how to treat their prisoners. However, after seeing how they all looked up to Tom and followed his lead, she knew she'd made the right decision. She could have never handled the situation at the ranch, and mistakes or not, Thomas Miller was Mercy's best chance of remaining free.

CHAPTER 8

CHLOE
Mercy, Montana

"IT SEEMS TOO QUIET OUT HERE," Ethan said as they neared the end of Main Street.

Chloe looked back at the empty farmers' market they'd just walked through and nodded in agreement. She couldn't remember the last time she'd seen the streets so bare, especially in the middle of the afternoon. While it was still overcast and breezy, the storm had moved on, leaving behind some debris and large puddles. "People are spooked."

"I don't blame them." Ethan ran a hand gingerly along his hairline, wincing as his fingers brushed one of the scratches. "I'm spooked, too."

Chloe tried to ignore the heavy feeling settling into her stomach, except she'd never been very good at pretending things were okay. Because they clearly weren't, and Ethan had been seriously off since the first time Chloe spotted him earlier with his dad. He was…evasive. Wouldn't look her in the eye. She got that he was freaked out and everything. If anyone could understand how he was feeling, it was her, only that didn't really matter if he wouldn't talk to her.

"You gonna tell me what happened?" she asked, getting straight to the point.

Ethan's step faltered slightly but he kept walking, staring straight ahead. "What do you mean, tell you what happened? You were there, Chloe. You saw it."

"I did more than see it," Chloe challenged. "I *killed* a guy before I ran away, Ethan. I'm pretty sure he was the one we listened to the whole afternoon while he died a slow and painful death."

Ethan jammed his hands deep into the pockets of his jeans and continued to keep his eyes fixed on the road ahead of them. "Yeah. I, um…didn't look at the first guy I shot, but I know he died."

"I thought you just clipped someone in the leg." Chloe stole a sideways glance and saw that he'd gone pale. He was breathing fast and his jaw was clenched so tight that he was sure to crack a couple of teeth. "Woah!" she said, taking him by the arm and forcing him to stop.

"No!" Ethan gasped, tearing his arm free and backing away. Raising his hands, he held them out like he was trying to talk someone down off a bridge. "Just…let it go. I…can't," he swallowed hard, his eyes wide and fearful.

Chloe recognized a panic attack when she saw one. She'd been fortunate enough not to suffer from crippling episodes herself, but she had a friend who did frequently. "Ethan," she said gently, not moving. "You're okay. You need to take a breath. Just breathe with me and you'll feel better." Slowly, she inhaled through her nose. "Like this."

Ethan focused on her mouth and began to mimic her motions, closing his eyes after releasing two shuddering breaths and taking a third.

"That's good." Chloe moved closer and gripped both of his hands in hers. "You're not alone, Ethan. We'll get through this. In the old world, we'd be put in therapy and probably medicated. Now, we'll just have to do the best we can, together."

"The nightmares were just starting to go away," he whispered, opening his eyes. The pain Chloe saw was so deep it was staggering.

"They'll go away again," she reassured him. "Tell ya what. Let's make a pact that we'll tell each other about our dreams every morning. That way, if we talk about them and acknowledge what it means and stuff, we can work through them faster."

"How do you know that?" he asked, already visibly relaxing.

Chloe shrugged. "Because I'm smart. I read things."

Ethan eyed her suspiciously. "You're making it up."

"Does it matter? Seriously, though, I read that talking about all the crap you've gone through, and the recurring dreams associated with it, helps your brain process the information." Chloe gave his hands an extra squeeze before dropping one of them, and then tugged on the other to get him moving again. "And we've both definitely been through some crap."

Ethan was silent for about half a block. "You were the first person I talked to about Decker and Billy and what happened with them. I did feel better afterward."

"See?" Chloe attempted a smile and was encouraged when he returned it. "Spreading the burden out makes it easier to carry."

Ethan raised his eyebrows at her. "Now you just sound weird." He moved closer so that their shoulders bumped and he grew serious. "But weird in a good way."

Chloe laughed lightly, her own intense emotions becoming more manageable. She hadn't allowed herself to unpack the experience yet and examine it from all the different angles, the way she normally would. When that happened, she knew it'd get ugly and she was going to need someone to turn to. Bishop, Sandy…even Crissy would be totally supportive. She knew that. But…there was something about having shared the experience that made Ethan the only person she could *really* talk to. Like, in a way that made sense.

Chloe squeezed his hand again and drew strength from the contact. In some bizarre way, the two of them now shared a bond that was both deep and horrible.

As they passed by City Hall, she considered distracting Ethan later with a "shopping" trip to the basement. She still wanted to show him the mysterious Q-Code, especially considering the latest developments.

"I saw that Crissy was finally reunited with Trevor," Ethan said, his voice sounding stronger as he talked about someone else.

Chloe rolled her eyes. "We'll be lucky to get her away from him long enough to help finish the hay. Honestly, though? It might be better that way. Even though Crissy got inside the house right after the shooting started and they never saw her, she's pretty traumatized."

"Dad said we've already got volunteers to start standing guard at the ranch," Ethan said, his face pinching up again. "Which is good, but I doubt it's necessary. Dillinger wouldn't bring his soldiers in on that trail, especially not after today. Bishop agrees. He thinks the corporal will come right up Main Street and make his demands."

"What'll happen when your dad says no?"

Ethan smiled broadly then, and Chloe wasn't sure she liked it. "The same as the last time he tried to steal from us, only this time he'll have more backup."

Madeline Stokes, the church pianist and all-around busybody, interrupted their conversation by banging open the front door of the church and bustling down the steps as they approached. Chloe wouldn't have guessed the woman could move that fast. As she turned in their direction, Madeline looked flustered and was absently pulling at her loose hair and touching her throat at the same time.

"Miss Stokes?" Ethan called to her when she kept walking without acknowledging them. "Is everything okay?"

Pausing about ten feet away, Madeline glanced over her shoulder at the church. "I, um…lit some candles. For those who lost their lives today."

Chloe waited for more of an explanation for her odd behavior, but Madeline simply shook her head at them and walked off without another word.

"That was strange," Chloe observed, watching her shuffle down the road.

"Miss Stokes has always been a little off," Ethan explained. "I mean, who would want to set up a vigil for a bunch of guys that came here to kill us?"

Chloe figured Ethan was probably right, except her gut was telling her there was more to the story. She couldn't shake the feeling as they climbed the steps and entered the large chamber. Expecting to see several candles lit, she was surprised to find the interior of the church dark, except for the filtered light coming through rows of stained glass windows.

As they approached the alter, Chloe could smell the telltale acrid odor of recently extinguished candles. A lot of them.

"Father Rogers!" Ethan called to the apparently empty nave. When there was no response, they headed for a partially open door to the side of the chancel. Ethan entered, while Chloe settled for poking her head inside. It was some sort of fancy office and there were several bookcases and ornate robes hanging up. "He isn't here," Ethan said to her, stating the obvious.

"Well, we tried." Chloe quickly walked back to the center of the church, in the middle of the pews. She didn't know why, but the place gave her the creeps. She had spent her fair share of time in churches and they usually had the opposite effect. "We'll let Patty know he isn't here."

"Let's try the apartment first," he suggested, walking past her and toward the back, where there was another opening opposite the office.

"Apartment?" Chloe frowned. "In a church?"

"The priest almost always lived in the church way back when," he explained with a grin. "Although, since they built the house behind this one, the apartment is usually used for Sunday school."

Chloe looked questioningly at him as they entered a dark hallway. Two doors on the right designated them as bathrooms, while the other doors on the left were marked for age groups… probably more Sunday school classes. "You sure know a lot about this place."

Ethan stopped in front of another door at the end of the hall and smirked. "Grandma Miller always made sure I came to church on Sundays when I was here for the weekend, and I've spent every Christmas break in Mercy. I *might* have been in a Christmas play or two." He paused with his hand raised to knock. "I wish I could have made it to the memorial for Father White last night, but we had too much work to do."

They both jumped back when the door abruptly jerked open. Father Rogers stood in the entrance, backlit by several burning candles. "I thought I heard talking out here." While his voice wasn't accusatory, it also wasn't friendly.

"Father Rogers!" Chloe said, moving forward and in front of

Ethan. "Mayor—I mean, Patty is looking for you. They need you at the clinic."

"Chloe, right?"

Chloe nodded once, thinking it was a strange response. "Yeah. We met before at the clinic. This is Ethan, he's—"

"You've got to be Tom's son," Russell interrupted, reaching out past Chloe to shake his hand. "Or I suppose I should say Mayor Miller, now."

"Yes, Father," Ethan answered hesitantly after taking the offered hand.

Father Rogers stepped back and ushered them inside. "You look just like him. Come in, I was just making some tea."

Tea? Chloe followed Ethan into the small kitchen area. It was too hot in the room, thanks to a strong fire in the woodstove. There was a teakettle on it, and the pastor went about getting more tea cups while he continued to speak.

"I heard that the men your father went after ended up at your place." Turning from the cupboard, Father Rogers set two cups on the table between them, not bothering to inquire if they even wanted any tea. "Tell me, how many people ended up dying today?"

"Eight," Ethan said flatly. "No one from Mercy."

"Hmm. I would have thought there would be more."

Chloe frowned at the man as he poured the water. He almost sounded…disappointed. What kind of priest was he?

"I heard you've already suffered a rather unfortunate series of events," Father Rogers continued, turning to Ethan and holding out one of the cups.

Ethan hesitated before taking it, staring back at the older man with a puzzled expression. "Yeah. I, uh, guess you could say that."

"Don't be modest," Father Rogers countered, tsking as he sat down in one of the chairs. Chloe took the other cup when he didn't offer it to her and remained standing.

"What?" Ethan asked, glancing over at Chloe.

"You see, Ethan, while I'm technically not a Catholic priest, people still have a need to confess their sins and that often times involves discussing the sins of others they're with." He took a small sip of tea and stared at Ethan over the rim of his cup. "I would imagine that after what you went through with Decker and Billy, today may have stirred up some bad emotions. Tell me, what was it like to be a part of taking a man's life? How did it feel?"

Chloe was stunned into silence. She stared open-mouthed at Ethan as he first looked confused, and then angry. "Sam," he muttered, before slamming the cup back down on the table.

Chloe knew Sam was rather religious and that he'd been to the church more than once already. He must be Catholic. While she couldn't blame Sam for trying to unburden his soul or whatever, she was totally baffled by the priest's violation in sharing it. Chloe wasn't Catholic, but even she knew that confessions were like, the ultimate secret.

"I've upset you," Father Rogers said, staring intensely at Ethan.

Setting her cup back on the table with enough force to spill the liquid, Chloe finally processed what had been said, and reacted accordingly. She'd never liked the guy, except before it was because she could tell he was being fake. This? Well, it was like the façade was gone, and she really didn't like what was behind it.

"We need to go," she said loudly.

"So soon?" Father Rogers grinned at her, finally looking away from Ethan.

His gaze was disturbing, and Chloe backed into Ethan as she met it and refused to turn away. There was a calculated coldness there, like a scientist with its subject instead of a sympathetic priest.

"Not soon enough," Ethan replied, and Chloe was impressed

with how controlled his voice was. "Should I tell Patty that you're *busy?*"

"Oh, but I am," Father Rogers called after them as they retreated back into the hall. "I have a much larger flock to tend to."

CHAPTER 9

ANNY

Miller Ranch, Mercy, Montana

"Thanks for getting me," Danny said, barely loud enough to be heard over the noise of the wagon. "Except I don't know if I agree with the decision that the wagon would be better for my head than horseback."

Tom grinned and then pulled on the reins, slowing them down. "Sorry, there's a lot of branches and other stuff in the road from all the wind."

It was growing dark, and Danny was having a hard time not being fearful of every little sound and movement she saw from the woods that lined the road. For as much of a fuss she made with Melissa about not wanting to stay the night at the clinic, she was glad that Tom was with her. "It was nice of your mom to bargain my release with the doc."

"She can pretty much talk anyone into whatever she wants," Tom said. He glanced at Danny with a look of concern. "I hope it was the smart thing to do, though. My mom's right that there are plenty of us to keep a close eye on you, and a nice bed, but what if you do have a concussion?"

"Honestly, Tom, even if I had a major head injury, there isn't a thing Melissa could do about it with the equipment and meds that she has." Danny pushed the gauze up out of her eyes again. The bulky bandage was wrapped all the way around her head and kept falling down into her face. She was okay with leaving it there for a few days, though. It was better than looking at her mangled ear. Not that she really cared about how it looked…her hair would cover most of it up. It was more the reminder that she almost had a bullet in her brain. Like, less than a half an inch away from it. She shuddered slightly and wrapped her arms around herself.

Tom must have noticed, because he scooted closer to her on the seat. Shifting both reins into his left hand, he draped his other arm over her shoulders. "I should have thought to bring a blanket."

Danny stiffened in response to his touch before she could stop herself, and then felt horrible when she saw him react. Slowly, Tom dropped his arm back down and shifted awkwardly on the hard bench seat. "My dad told me the repeater was intentionally destroyed," she said, trying to cover up her behavior.

Tom gave her a questioning look before nodding. "Yeah, like we suspected. There's no doubt now this is all coordinated. I've got both Caleb and Bishop on their radios, trying to glean any sort of related communications."

Glad for the distraction, Danny eagerly dove into the conversation. "Does anyone else know about the second radio?"

"We told Sheriff Waters," Tom said, his voice growing irritated. "While I didn't exactly lie to him about it, I left him with the impression that Bishop voluntarily told me, and that he only recently got it working."

Danny frowned. "And the truth?" It was the first chance they'd had to talk about anything alone since he'd left the day before.

"The truth is that I caught him up in that room two days ago, and after my face got real cozy with the floor, he fessed up to fixing it a while ago. Probably more than a week."

Danny frowned at him, and winced at the pain it caused. "Bishop put *you* down?"

Tom shrugged. "Guy's got some advanced training, Danny. That's why even though I believe him when he says he's trying to look out for us, I know there's a lot more he isn't saying. And I don't like that."

"Well, I didn't find much." When he turned and looked at her in surprise, she widened her eyes at him. "What? I told you I'd go through his stuff, and I did. The papers in the radio room make it sound like he's trying to find the kids' parents. Then there was some other stuff I couldn't decipher. A bunch of broken up sentences about the Duke Ranch and some military jargon. Nothing that I would consider necessarily suspicious."

"And his room?"

"First of all, you should tell Sam to wash his socks." Smiling at Tom, Danny noticed that he had managed to slide over to his original position on the seat, so their bodies weren't touching anymore. She was frustrated by the conflicting emotions welling up—relief that he wasn't pushing things and also a profound need to feel his touch. Danny knew she was at risk of shutting down again. It was so much safer...easier that way. Her voice faltered as she struggled to keep talking, horrified that she was on the verge of unexpected tears.

Tom was staring at her. "Are you okay?"

Gritting her teeth, she turned away and kept talking. "He had a picture in his bag of him and a young man. I think it might be his son. The only other thing even marginally interesting was an engraved compass. Did you know he was a colonel in the military and that his last name is Campbell?"

"Campbell?" Tom looked perplexed. "I thought it was Kingston. Pretty sure that's what my mom said. I already knew he was in the military, except he made it sound like it was a little time in the state guard. A colonel is a high-ranking officer."

"I suppose the compass could have belonged to someone else. Maybe it's a family heirloom or something," Danny suggested.

"No." Tom sounded sure of himself. "I think it's his, and I think there's a lot more to the story. I'm hoping he'll trust us enough to let us in on it. There might be a way to use his knowledge or connections to help us."

"With Dillinger?"

Tom looked at her again, his face becoming more difficult to see in the gathering shadows. "Yeah, with Dillinger."

They rode in silence for several minutes as the wagon wheels clambered over the road. "You can't blame yourself for what's happening." Danny knew she was pushing it, but suddenly decided to get it all out on the table. Tom meant too much to her.

"Why not?" he answered quickly, and with some heat. "You do."

Danny swallowed. She felt like such a jerk. Reaching out, she took the reins from his hands and pulled the horses to a stop. "Tom!" she shouted, when he moved like he was going to jump down from the wagon.

He froze, and slowly turned to face her. He looked defeated and her breath caught, making it impossible to talk. "I know, I did it again," he said, grimacing. "First when I attacked and nearly killed you, then when I acted impulsively with Dillinger, which is now coming back to haunt us all, and yesterday when I ran off to chase after my own demons, leaving you defenseless." He reached out then and gently touched the bandage on her head. "I don't blame you for not wanting me to touch you."

"Tom," she said again, this time with compassion. Taking his hand from her damaged face, she held on tight to make sure he wouldn't try and run off before she finished what she had to say. "I don't blame you."

He didn't look convinced.

Taking a deep breath, Danny did one of the most terrifying things of her life; she let him in. Her eyes welling, she moved across the seat. "I could never blame you for loving your son so thoroughly that you would sacrifice *anything* for him, or so proud that you'd never let a coward like Dillinger control you. How could I hate you for wanting to protect Mercy? Yes, you're impulsive, and hard-headed, and sometimes you infuriate me, but… that's also why I love you."

Tom stared at her and she held her breath, willing him to believe her. Praying that she didn't just make the worst mistake of her—

Tom pulled Danny against him, careful not to bump her head. His arms encircled her in an embrace she used to think she would never long for, and now wanted more than anything. She got lost in the sensation of being the same in body and soul, and numbly wondered if that was what it felt like to be in love.

Pulling back just enough so he could bring his lips close to hers, Tom whispered into her good ear. "Thank you for trusting me, Danny. I was going to always love you no matter what, so it's a good thing we both feel the same way."

Laughing, Danny brought her lips to his and in that moment, their world was okay.

CHAPTER 10

GENERAL MONTGOMERY
Cheyenne Mountain Complex, Colorado

THE TWO REMAINING joint commanders both appeared uncomfortable as they looked up at General Montgomery when he entered his office. They sat next to each other at the large conference table, a stack of papers and coffee that had likely gone cold in front of them. Montgomery had intentionally kept them waiting. Just because the end of known civilization was upon them didn't mean he had to abandon good powerplay tactics.

"Sorry to keep you waiting," he lied, pulling out a chair opposite the military leaders. Montgomery sat without offering an explanation and then looked expectantly at Walsh, who was hovering nervously at the far end of the room. His assistant was continuing to slowly unravel and he knew the day would soon come when he'd have to cut him loose. If the man could keep it together for just one more week, they'd be in a much stronger position. Dillinger was about to deliver, and he could then use the combined success of Monida, the Duke Ranch in Graham's Place, and Miller Ranch in Mercy as examples of what could be accomplished. Once a greater plan was established, he'd move forward with implementing the strategy in the remaining states, and Walsh could finish having his breakdown. But not yet.

"Um, right. The first order of business will be our latest numbers and estimates, which were just finalized," Walsh stammered. "If you'll look at the top sheet—"

"That's it?" Sergeant Major O'Shane interrupted. "We're going to completely gloss over the fact that we haven't met for more than a week, or even recognize the death of Vice Admiral Baker?"

"I would have thought the memorial was recognition enough," Major General Visor said, turning to the sergeant beside him. "I'm quite certain we'll be discussing his replacement. Right, General?" he asked, looking back to Montgomery.

General Montgomery carefully gauged his reaction. He still needed both the Army and Marine commanders support. "I thought it might be in poor taste to open our meeting today by speaking about the Admiral's death and the need to thrust someone into his position. But certainly, Sergeant, we can get right to the meat of things. Hmm? If you pull out the bottom paper, you will see the valid candidates brought forward by myself as well as the both of you. While it will be impossible to truly replace Admiral Baker, I believe any of these applicants will be adequate. I propose we take some time to look them over and then meet to vote on it in a couple of days."

Sergeant O'Shane blushed as he shuffled his papers around, clearly wanting to say something more. "General Montgomery, you know full well that isn't what I meant."

Walsh cleared his throat. "There is also a copy of the investigation into his cause of death."

"He died a hero on the battlefield," Montgomery interjected. "What more is there to say?"

Sergeant O'Shane glanced first at Visor and then Walsh, before settling on Montgomery. "No, I don't suppose there is."

"Then let's get on with it." Standing, Montgomery walked to the end of the table where a carafe sat, and poured himself a cup of fresh coffee. "I'm sure you are well aware, Sergeant, of the death toll, considering your work with the science team."

"Unfortunately, I am." Running a hand through his graying hair, Sergeant O'Shane went back to the top page on the pile. Although he wasn't yet fifty, Montgomery noticed how the man appeared to have aged drastically over the past few weeks. "The original estimate from eleven days ago put us at around sixty-five million survivors," O'Shane reported. "And another twenty-five percent are expected to succumb to other factors in the next month. With the horrific storms ravaging the West Coast as well as the bacterial outbreak, our newest projections are fifty million."

"Fifty million as the anticipated final tally when this all settles?" Major Visor asked.

"No," Walsh answered. "As our current population, and that is likely optimistic."

Visor paled and he started to scribble numbers on the back of the paper. "But that's…that has to be a death rate of—"

"Eighty-five percent," O'Shane interjected, doing the math for him. "We still haven't gotten the final death tolls from the latest storms, but we all know that in addition to the direct casualties, we also have tens of thousands of new refugees fleeing the coast. This additional burden will likely overrun and collapse some of the FEMA camps that have been recently established in the western states."

"In a few more months, especially after winter, we can expect that number to climb to ninety percent," Walsh added. He sounded as depressed as he looked and Montgomery glared at him. He needed him to be composed and confident.

"What can we do?" Major Visor splayed his hands out on the table and leaned forward in earnest. "There has to be more that we can do!"

General Montgomery nodded at Visor as he walked with his coffee to stand in front of the giant map. "Sometimes, a physician can spend so much time trying to address the patient's body as a whole in order to save him that he fails to see the obvious. So, instead of cutting off the festering limb and healing what is left, the infection is left to spread, killing the patient."

"General?" Visor said almost pleadingly, clearly not getting the point.

Turning to face them, the general was grim. "It's time to focus on what we can do, rather than what we cannot. I was hopeful that our reach would be strong enough to encompass *everyone* that is left. However, it has become apparent that the changing weather and continued losses on the ground will hammer us until nothing remains, if we don't take advantage of what is working."

Walsh jumped to his feet and Montgomery was pleased with his timing. As he watched his assistant handing the commanders the appropriate reports, he was encouraged that perhaps the colonel could still be useful, after all.

"FEMA Shelter M3 continues to thrive," Montgomery began, remaining in front of the map. "The new command center at the Duke Ranch is functioning beyond expectations and is quite promising for the community of Graham's Place, despite some local dissent. The mountain town of Mercy is our next point of interest," he continued, approaching the map and pointing out the green tack. "We've been told of an impressive cattle ranch there with more than a thousand cows, and it is perfectly positioned for yet another command."

O'Shane skimmed over the paper Walsh had given him. "You're suggesting we pull back our farther-reaching efforts and concentrate on creating more of these 'communities'," he surmised.

Major Visor was nodding, and some of his color was coming back. "This is promising. What is the farming project mentioned here? Do you really feel confident of our ability to feed upwards of several *million* in the coming year?"

Montgomery glanced at Walsh to confirm his reaction wasn't questionable. When he managed to keep a neutral expression, the general walked back to the table and sat down, folding his hands in front of him in a relaxed manner. "I would like to assure both of you that while some of my tactics might seem radical, they are for good reasons. Focusing on petty political squabbles while hundreds of thousands more are dying would be inexcusable. So, you will have to forgive me for focusing on the long-term survivability for the largest, while still realistic numbers."

The general paused, giving the other commanders an opportunity to interrupt him if they were strongly opposed to anything he'd already said. When they remained silent, he sat up straighter in his chair and continued. "I am still waiting on confirmation from Corporal Dillinger, and fully expect some other aspects of the mentioned project to be worked out soon. While I don't want to raise false hope, I will tell you that my seemingly unconnected maneuvers over the past three weeks have been geared towards locating and facilitating a top-secret program that will all but guarantee that these isolated communities can flourish."

"And the rest of the country?" Sergeant O'Shane asked, though not in an accusatory manner.

"Think of these small groups, overseen by the military, as our final attempt at addressing the needs of the nation systemically," General Montgomery said, steepling his fingers. "My hope is that, once successful, the approach can be replicated until it includes everyone."

Major Visor was nodding again, looking relieved. He even went so far as to reach out and grip O'Shane's forearm. "You've told me what the science team has been forecasting," he said. "If anyone can appreciate what the general is trying to do, I'd think it would be you."

Sergeant O'Shane stood and carefully stacked his papers, tapping them down until the edges were all aligned before looking up to meet the general's intense stare. "If you can, in fact, successfully demonstrate these towns working cohesively with our military, and give valid details on whatever this program is, I will guarantee the backing of our Marine forces."

"And I the Army," Visor said eagerly.

The general offered a small, compensatory smile before the other officers left the room. As the door swung shut, he turned to Walsh, a scowl clouding his features. "Anything new from Dillinger?"

"Um, no sir." Walsh glanced furtively at the empty chairs and back to Montgomery. "You don't think we should have told them everything?"

Montgomery closed his eyes and forced himself to take a breath before answering. "Colonel, there are times when I can't help but question where your loyalties are."

"They lie with the people, sir."

Slamming his hands down on the table, the general stood with enough force to nearly topple his chair. "Don't you dare question where my loyalties are."

"I wasn't, sir," Walsh answered with a surprising amount of calm. "I was merely defending myself. You are the one raising the question of who is and is not loyal to our sworn oath."

Taken aback for a moment, Montgomery shook his head to

clear it. They were getting distracted by petty bickering and he refused to waste any more time. "How about 1ˢᵗ Force Recon?"

"Still dark."

"Dr. Watson?" Montgomery asked. He circled around to his desk and sat down at it, frustrated with the roadblocks.

"Cooperating, now that we've got her granddaughter happy. In fact, we've narrowed down a couple of likely areas for the vaults." Walsh looked distraught, rather than optimistic, as he pushed a folder across the general's desk.

"I thought she didn't know." Picking the folder up, Montgomery opened it.

"She wasn't sure," Walsh confirmed. "But it turns out she always had her suspicions and now that she understands the full scope of what is occurring, she's rather enthusiastic about heading up the farming program."

"The colonel in charge of the vault project was living in rural Montana," Montgomery muttered while looking over the short list. They were all locations in either Oregon or Montana. He sat the folder back down and drummed on it with his fingers while staring absently up at the map. "Where should Dillinger be now?"

Walsh frowned. "We last heard directly from him when he was at the Pony Express station near Helena. We don't expect anything for another day or two, after they've reached Mercy."

"Is the team at Malmstrom on standby?"

"Already sent," Walsh confirmed.

"Good. I'm tired of waiting, and I don't trust Dillinger on his own. We can't afford to let Mercy turn into a bloodbath." Standing, Montgomery held the folder back out to Walsh. "Is that piece of crap Huey Dillinger was using back here and operational?"

Walsh's frown deepened. "Yes, sir, but—"

"Have it ready to spin up at fifteen hundred hours." Montgomery tugged at his uniform. Dillinger was an idiot, and he needed to keep a shorter leash on his pitbull. He couldn't afford any mistakes, not when so much was at stake. "Meet me on the tarmac then with Dr. Watson."

"Sir?" Walsh asked, confused.

"It's imperative that we have the continued support of both the Army and Marine commanders," Montgomery said, irritated he had to explain the obvious. He would personally oversee Dillinger's handling of Mercy, and it was clear that the geneticist could better serve them in Montana. "We're going to the Duke Ranch," he announced. "It's time we paid a visit to Command Center Two." Perhaps he'd leave Walsh there with the doctor as a show of his continued presence.

Smiling for the first time that day, Montgomery headed for the door. He had some packing to do.

CHAPTER 11

TOM

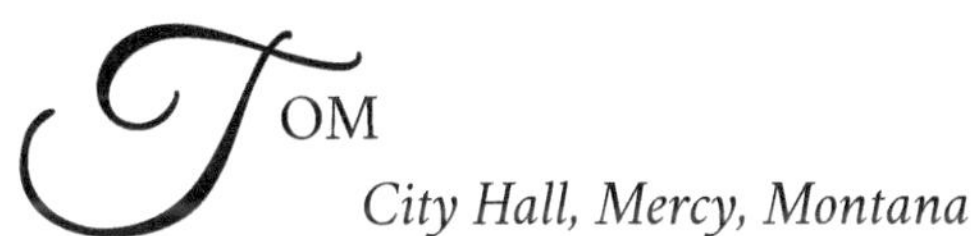

City Hall, Mercy, Montana

TOM MADE sure he was already seated before everyone began arriving. He knew his size could make him intimidating, and that wasn't how he wanted to control the meeting. Patty somehow managed to have fresh coffee and some sort of pastry to offer as a breakfast already spread out on the table. Something Tom would have never thought to do. He still had a lot to learn.

Bishop's voice was rising again so Tom shot him a cautionary glare. While he appreciated how he'd started things off by explaining the second radio and news about the Duke Ranch, Bishop wasn't handling the pushback very well. Maybe, if he had given the town leaders the full story, there wouldn't be so many questions.

Tom didn't say anything when Bishop failed to mention his military background, or how long he'd really been using the radio. However, he planned on having a long, detailed conversation with the guy later that night, back at the ranch. Tom wasn't going to accept any more excuses. It was time for the full story. On everything.

"Let him talk," Tom finally said, interrupting Bishop as he attempted to argue with Gary. He was annoying, and had been going out of his way to cause trouble, but he was still a councilman. Gary also had a legitimate point that others in the room were likely thinking, and just not saying. It was best to get it all out in the open.

"Right," Gary fumbled, clearly not expecting Tom to encourage him. "Well, okay. I just can't help but wonder if Tom is what's best for Mercy right now. Would Dillinger even be motivated to come here if it wasn't for his interaction with you and your group at the FEMA camp?" he asked, looking pointedly at Tom. He gained confidence as he spoke, his voice rising. "And how about the detailed map you left for him at the Duke Ranch, which literally showed him exactly where to go!"

Tom shifted in his seat and bit back his initial reaction. He hoped no one noticed how he was clenching his jaw, or how he was sitting on his hands. "What do you want me to say, Gary? That this is all my fault? Fine, if that's what it'll take for us to move beyond it. It's all my—"

"No." Patty stood as she spoke, sounding harsh. Waving a hand in the air over her head, she made a grand motion to include everyone in the room. "We're not doing this. If we start sitting around this table, pointing fingers and blaming each other for everything that goes wrong, we'll never get around to doing something about it!"

It was still pretty early in the morning, and Tom had noticed a couple of people in attendance had begun to look distracted. Patty definitely had a way to snap everyone back to attention and he was glad she was on his side. She may have handed off the torch for running the town but she continued to be very much an influential figure.

"Is this Dillinger guy coming sooner than he would have?" Sheriff Waters said as Patty took her seat. "Maybe. That doesn't mean the military wouldn't have come knocking eventually. And I don't see how we can blame Tom for another man's actions. If we're looking for someone to blame, I think we should start with whoever gave the order for those outlaws to attack us. Or, how about whoever's pulling the strings behind Dillinger?"

"He's right." Paul pushed his chair back, the scraping sound underscoring his words. Everyone looked at him in surprise. Tom knew he was Gary's best friend and he was the last person anyone expected to speak out against Gary, or in support of Tom.

Standing, Paul looked down pleadingly at Gary, who was seated next to him. "You know how much I've lost. As much or more than anyone in this room. Gary, I saw Tom yesterday." Turning from his friend, he stared at Tom. "I heard those first shots from my place and rode over as fast as I could. I don't know what I could have done to help if I'd gotten there sooner, but…well, I still went. I got there a few minutes behind y'all, and things were already under control. I saw Tom fighting those men," he continued, addressing the rest of the room. "I saw a man willing to do whatever it took to save his family, his farm, *and* his town. So, I say let Dillinger come. Tom dealt with him once before and I'm sure we can all figure out a way to successfully deal with him here in Mercy, too."

As Paul re-took his seat, Tom cleared his throat. "I appreciate that, Paul. And while I understand your concerns, Gary, I also think the sheriff has a valid point. I might have inadvertently sped up our clash with the military, which I regret, but it was coming nonetheless. They want our cattle. Not just mine, either, but all of ours. They want our crops, our medical supplies, and our farms. They want our *town*, regardless of who's here."

"What are we going to do about it?" Mr. Sullivan asked. Tom sighed inwardly in relief. Another bullet dodged and they seemed to be moving on to more solid ground.

"Get as much information as we can," Sam answered as he stood and went to the white board. He was obviously in his element and Tom smiled appreciatively at his friend. Sam already had several things written out on the board in preparation, which he addressed one-by-one as he spoke. "First, Caleb and Bishop will both spend extra time on the radios, trying to make contact with other FEMA shelters and military bases. Our hope is that Dillinger might be acting on his own, without any direct orders. Or, if he does have orders, we might be able to get someone else in a higher position to oppose it. Second, we were successful in our interrogation this morning with the, umm, prisoner. He confirmed the outlaws were acting on behalf of Corporal Dillinger and that their primary objectives were to take the cattle and attack the farm. Third, we propose that tomorrow we use the city barbeque and Fourth of July celebration as a time to inform the town as to what is and has been happening, and to request volunteers to act as our own form of city guard."

"Who's going to train them?" Dr. Olsen didn't look convinced, though Tom was relieved to see that most of the others in attendance were nodding in approval of the plan.

"I will," Sheriff Waters replied. "I have military as well as some SWAT training. Bishop has offered to assist me, and I know there are several other veterans living in Mercy, including Caleb."

Caleb gave a salute to the sheriff from his spot at the end of the table. "Yes, sir. Over twenty years in the Army. I imagine I still recall a thing or two."

Several more gestures of approval, including Fire Chief Martinez and Councilwoman Betty. Tom wished Danny could have been there, but his mom insisted that no one wake her that morning. She had opted to stay behind with her and the kids, so they could all get back to cutting the hay. They had four people from town voluntarily standing guard, plus the radios were working again, thanks to Tane and his quick repair job. Tom didn't think he could stomach being separated again if they didn't have the ability to communicate.

"I feel better knowing we have a plan," Al commented, scratching at the stubble on his jaw. The gas station owner frowned as he pointed at Sam and the board. "I'm just not so sure it's a good idea to be throwing a party tomorrow, considering everything that's going on."

"Actually," Melissa said, looking more optimistic. "While I'm not a psychiatrist, I know enough about mental health to say that I think it would be good for everyone to go forward with the barbeque. It's one of the few constants we've had to look forward to. Not to mention the fact that a whole lot of people are lacking in getting enough protein. Everyone needs to eat, no matter what else is happening."

"And I think it's an appropriate celebration," Patty added.

"I think it is, too," Tom said, finally standing. As all eyes turned in his direction, he offered a silent prayer that he'd choose the right words. He wasn't all that good at speeches; physical confrontations were more his thing. "The Fourth of July is all about celebrating our independence. It might come across as a little ironic to be making a recruiting speech during it for the possible need to go up against our own military, but it's about maintaining Mercy's freedom. The God-given right to not have your freedom or property taken from you, no matter who it is that's trying to do it."

When no one challenged him, and even Gary looked as if he might agree, Tom was encouraged to continue. "This afternoon, I'll be overseeing the slaughter of one of our cows so we can all come together tomorrow, as a town, and celebrate our continued survival. The only way we're going to succeed is by doing it together. Now, I'm certainly not looking to pick a fight with our military. I think we're all in agreement that our goal is to protect Mercy, and to look for a way to work alongside what remains of our country in a way that benefits everyone, while ensuring our continued freedom."

Bishop was the first to clap, and Tom's initial reaction was to frown at him. However, as one person after another joined in, and then began to stand with Tom, he understood that something important was happening. Something that went beyond giving a speech to make people happy. It was a truth and a common goal that they all shared. It was about more than simply surviving. It was about thriving as a community, together, because they were all a part of something bigger than themselves.

Tom found himself compelled to join them and was caught up in the applause until the sounds all merged into one.

CHAPTER 12

USSELL
Mercy Parish, Mercy, Montana

RUSSELL SET his pack on the wooden chair next to the small kitchen table and placed a bag of beef jerky inside, on top of the other things he'd already packed. His bike was hidden up near the spring, something he'd managed to accomplish the day before when everyone was distracted by the attack on the ranch. Not that he really cared if anyone knew he was leaving; he was free to depart Mercy whenever he chose. He simply preferred to avoid questions, and drawing any sort of attention to himself would limit his ability to move around unfettered.

A rare look of discontent crossed his handsome features as Russell recalled the conversation with Ethan and Chloe from the day before. It was rather unfortunate, but the boy had a way of drawing out his curiosity. He simply couldn't resist evoking the desired reactions, even though it could potentially disrupt the façade he'd been successfully presenting. Russell scoffed at himself as he gathered the last few items lying on the table. It didn't matter anymore if someone found him odd. After tomorrow, Mercy would be nothing more than another memory. One stop among many along Russell's route.

He paused to examine the Glock, badge, and nametag belonging to Deputy Rogers. If he had to take on another persona again, Russell would certainly opt for the role of a police officer, instead of a pastor. He decided pastoring required too much patience.

An urgent knocking at the back door disrupted his thoughts, and Russell quickly stuffed the gun and other objects into the backpack before going to answer it. Hovering on the porch, looking somewhat lost, was Councilman Gary.

"Gary," Russell said without a lot of enthusiasm. "What brings you here?"

"I need to talk to you," Gary pled, literally pushing his way past Russell and into the kitchen.

"Have you come to confess your sins?" Though irritated by the intrusion, Russell still found the groveling worm to be amusing.

Gary waved a hand absently, completely missing the satire in the comment. "No, no. You were right about the leaders of this town and how they have their own agendas. Something needs to be done about Thomas Miller. Patty has him wrapped around her finger and how no one else sees he is nothing more than her puppet, I'll never understand. Please, Father," he continued emphatically. "People might listen to you."

"Why don't you call me Russell, since we seem to be such dear friends."

"O-Okay," Gary stammered, wavering in his resolve at the realization that Russell wasn't taking him seriously. "I thought you were one of the few here who saw clearly what Patty's been doing. Now, things are even worse with Tom. He acts like he's

John Wayne, here to save the day, when all he's really doing is bringing more misery."

"Yes, Tom," Russell muttered. Gary was right that the man had a superiority complex, though perhaps not completely unwarranted. Ethan bore a close resemblance to his father, and they both reminded Russell of his own brother. Was that why he found himself so intrigued by the boy?

"Did you know the Pony Express station may have been attacked?" Gary was asking. "Now some corporal Tom got in a fight with is probably going to turn Mercy into a FEMA camp and of course, Tom wants to fight him instead."

Gary had left the door open in his haste and a gust of wind found its way inside, snuffing out the candle on the table. As the smoke rose and Russell tuned out the other man's incessant dialog, he compared Ethan's features with what remained of the memory of his younger brother. It was a mistake.

The kitchen faded, to be replaced with the small attic room of his childhood, heavy with the smell of burning candles. "Edelweiss" was playing, the tune clunky and erratic as the player's teeth bounced over the plastic disc.

Daniel was there. A constant pest even though Russell was exceptionally cruel to him. He was particularly persistent that day in trying to get his older brother's attention, and had entered Russell's room knowing he would pay dearly for it. He told Daniel to go away. He had warned him. But instead, the ten-year-old did the one thing he knew would make his big brother react. He snatched the blue plastic disc from the player and stood there holding it at the top of the stairs, a grin on his face.

Russell didn't remember being mad. Instead, he'd felt a calm unlike anything he'd ever experienced as he approached his younger brother and without comment, shoved him down the stairs. The house was old and the stairs were steep, and Daniel's small body appeared to fly for the briefest of moments as he toppled head over heels, to land in an unmoving heap at the bottom. That was where their mother discovered him, dead, several hours later. Russell was sitting on his bed, listening to Edelweiss over and over again. Russell was just twelve years old, and it was the first time he'd taken a life.

"Father?"

Russell blinked, his mind still drifting in the dark, stuffy attic room.

"Russell?" Gary's voice rose as his concern grew over the blank stare and unresponsive nature of the priest. Reaching out, he grabbed at Russell's arms to give him a shake. "Are you okay?"

Russell reacted to the physical contact as if he'd been touched with hot irons, jumping back and colliding with the chair he was standing next to. The backpack toppled over and onto the floor, some of its contents spilling out and clattering across the wooden boards.

His head slowly clearing, Russell was at first simply annoyed with both himself and Gary. He didn't welcome the imposition of either the visit or the memory it had provoked. The lapse of control was a rare occurrence and not something often witnessed. It seemed to be happening more often since coming to Mercy. Another compelling reason to leave.

Gary still stood awkwardly in the middle of the kitchen, glancing back and forth between the floor and Russell. He didn't understand what had the idiot so baffled until Gary knelt down and pointed at the gun on the floor.

"Wha-what's this?" he stuttered, looking up at Russell, his eyes wide.

"The road is a dangerous place for anyone to be," Russell said evenly, and then sighed when Gary continued to go through his things. Really, the man was getting to be an increasingly maddening nuisance.

Ignoring the beef jerky and two pairs of rolled-up socks, Gary chose to pick up the police badge and nametag. "Deputy Rogers," Gary read aloud as he stood with the curious evidence in his hands. "Why do you have this?"

Russell smiled warmly as he reached out and gently removed the gun from Gary's hand. Tsking, he shook his head as he stepped around the other man. "Oh, Gary." Moving to the door, Russell closed it firmly before turning around, the smile gone from his face. "I really wish you hadn't seen that."

CHAPTER 13

ETHAN
Miller Ranch, Mercy, Montana

ETHAN RESTED his arms on the top rail of the lodge-pole fence and leaned against it. Sam sat next to him, balanced on the pole with his feet resting on the bottom pine railing. They were both scrutinizing the butchering of a cow that was taking place nearby.

The location had been carefully chosen to make the transportation of the meat easier. They were a fair distance away from the barn and main field, and next to the road leading into the ranch, so the wagons could be pulled up close. There'd been a brief debate about simply leading the cow all the way into town before shooting it, but in the end, his dad determined what he thought was the best way to go about it.

Fortunately, the weather was cooperating for the time being. Ethan was getting used to the unpredictable nature of it though, so he knew the currently innocent-looking clouds scattered to

78

the east could easily morph into something entirely different by nightfall. He sniffed at the air, and was comforted that it at least smelled the same, a mixture of dry grass, cow dung, and good ol' Montana dirt.

Brushing some of that dirt from his hands, Ethan was thankful to get a break from cutting the never-ending hayfield. He'd been pleasantly surprised earlier when Sam arrived back from the town meeting just before lunch, with a group of volunteers to help speed things along. Ten of them in all, which was more than enough manpower to finish the harvest by the end of the day.

Sandy was currently doing an expert job of directing them, and was already organizing another workforce to do something similar at several other farms in the valley. Sort of like an old-fashioned barn raising, only for harvesting, instead.

Ethan was glad to have a few minutes alone with Sam because he wanted to let him know about the disturbing conversation with Russell from the day before. He'd had time to process it while cutting grass that morning, and just laid it all out for him. Ethan chewed on a piece of straw while waiting for his friend's reaction.

Running a hand through his salt-and-pepper hair, Sam cursed under his breath before turning to look down at Ethan. His face was noticeably flushed, which was saying a lot considering his Hispanic complexion. "I'm afraid that poor excuse for a priest *did* get his information from me. I thought it was a confidential way for me to talk through some things. I can't—" Sam stopped and wiped the back of his hand across his mouth. "I spoke about a lot more than you, Ethan. There were some heavy things on my heart regarding my wife, and I never thought my trust would be violated in such a way. I hope you can forgive me."

Ethan immediately regretted telling him. His goal wasn't to make Sam feel bad, and there really wasn't anything to be done about it. "Oh, jeez, Sam…it's not *your* fault. I'm not mad at you about it, so you don't need to apologize to me. I just thought you'd want to know you can't trust the guy. I'm sorry if I upset you."

Sam jumped down from the fence and began to pace. "So, we'll agree that neither of us needs to apologize to the other. You know what? I feel the deep need for another confession coming on."

Ethan smirked, relieved that Sam was able to keep a sense of humor about it. Except he hoped he wasn't serious. The last thing Ethan wanted was to be in the middle of yet more drama. "Don't you think we already have enough to fight about right now?" he asked, raising an eyebrow at Sam.

Sam stopped his marching and shook his head. "I suppose you're right, but something needs to be said about Father Russell. Maybe I'll corner Patty tomorrow after the barbeque. I think she's on some sort of church committee. It's a serious breach of etiquette that they need to be made aware of."

"How's the whole indoor farming going?" Ethan asked, eager to change the subject. "Anyone come up with some other sites yet? I know Henry's Hollow is big, but it won't be enough for everything we'll need."

"You're absolutely right," Sam confirmed, leaning back against the fence beside him. "It's going to come down to a combination of existing greenhouses, barns, and a couple of caves. At this point, I don't think it'll be a lack of growing space that will be our greatest challenge."

"Water?" Ethan guessed.

"Nope." Sam narrowed his eyes at him. "Guess again."

"Dirt?"

Sam laughed. "Dirt is the one thing we have plenty of. No, it'll be finding an adequate supply of what we need to plant. We simply don't have enough seeds, and with the acid rain already having an impact, I'm concerned what our success rate will be. It'll be hard enough to overcome our lack of artificial sunlight."

Ethan was at a loss as far as having anything intelligent to add. "We'll be working on our water problem here once the hay is done, but then Chloe and I should be able to help with the cave. At least, for a little while."

"Cleanup won't even start for a couple of more days," Sam said, kicking at a clump of soil. "We need to wait until we have a better grasp on what's happening outside of Mercy before we get too many people tied up inside the mountain."

Ethan found it frustrating that they were having to delay important work because of Dillinger. He wished he could have thought of a way to sabotage him back when he had basically free range at the FEMA shelter. Of course, he had no way of knowing then that the guy would come back to haunt them.

A rapid string of barks caused both Ethan and Sam to turn away from the fence. Grace came bounding across the grass towards them, tongue lolling. The retriever loved farm life and although she was constantly running around, had even managed to fatten up to a healthier weight. Ethan knelt down to greet her, only to be bowled over by the dog. "Hey!" he grunted as he fell onto his back, trying to fend off his excited friend. "Down, Grace! Ugh, that's enough tongue."

Sam laughed as Ethan struggled, not offering any help. "That's what you get for not taking her on a walk last night."

"I was busy," Ethan muttered as he staggered to his feet. "I was finally beating Chloe at Risk. No way could I walk away from that."

"And who ended up winning?" Sam gave a wink, not expecting an answer.

The sounds of an approaching wagon spared Ethan the need to make up any more excuses, and he smiled when he saw that it was Danny and Chloe. It had been nice having both Grace and

Danny around the farm and he hoped they'd stay longer. He understood why she wanted to be with her dad, of course. He also knew how small Tane's house was, so there was always a chance of the ranch luring her.

"Think they're ready for us yet?" Danny called out as they pulled up.

Sam scratched at his head and gestured down to where Tom and four other men and a woman were gathered. "I'm not much of a judge, but it sure looks like they've got some pieces piling up."

Chloe grimaced and Ethan tried not to laugh at her expression. "You sure you want to be a part of this?" he asked.

Straightening on the wooden seat next to Danny, she set her lips in a thin line. "Absolutely. I need to learn about this stuff if I ever hope to call myself a farmer, and I will do whatever it takes at this point to get me out of that hayfield."

Ethan noticed she was wearing her custom Star Wars tank top, and for some reason it gave him a sense of contentment. He'd given it and all of his other clothes she'd been wearing back to her, since most didn't even fit him anymore. They'd come to a mutual understanding about most of it, except he still suspected she'd been using his toothbrush, though she passionately denied it.

"Great timing!" Tom called out as he trudged up the sloped ground to where they were gathered. "If you pull the wagon up around the corner, there's a smaller dirt road you can use to get closer." His hands were covered in blood and there were flecks of it splattered on his jeans, making him look like some character out of a backwoods slasher film.

"So long as you guys do all the loading and unloading, I am happy to drive this wagon," Danny offered, smiling warmly at Tom even though her head was still thick with bandages and she looked like someone who'd been in a war.

Watching the exchange, and the way his dad responded by looking away, almost…shyly, Ethan got the sense that something had changed between the two. He grinned. If things were going that well between his dad and Danny, that might mean a better chance of her staying there. Which meant Grace would stay, too.

He waved at Chloe when the wagon started moving again as his dad led them to the other road. Ethan was cautiously hopeful. It felt right, all of them together again. Except he knew that just like when they were on the road, nothing was certain anymore and it could all change quickly.

Sam told him they were basically in a wait-and-see situation. They were monitoring the radios, and the riders who continued on to the Pony Express station two days ago should be coming back anytime to give a report. Hopefully, after his dad's recruiting announcement at the barbeque the next day, they'd have enough volunteers to get some good patrols going so they at least wouldn't be an easy target.

Meanwhile, Ethan was eager to move forward. He needed to keep busy or else his thoughts had too much time to turn inward.

"Break's over," Sam said, slapping Ethan on the back. "If we don't get back to that field, your grandmother will have us slinging cow dung for the next two days straight."

Ethan watched Grace chase after the wagon before turning to follow Sam. He only made it a few feet before he paused and looked up at the clouds to the east he'd spotted earlier. Sure enough, they were already changing. Much like the other threats looming over them, they were beginning to cast a shadow as they steadily crawled closer.

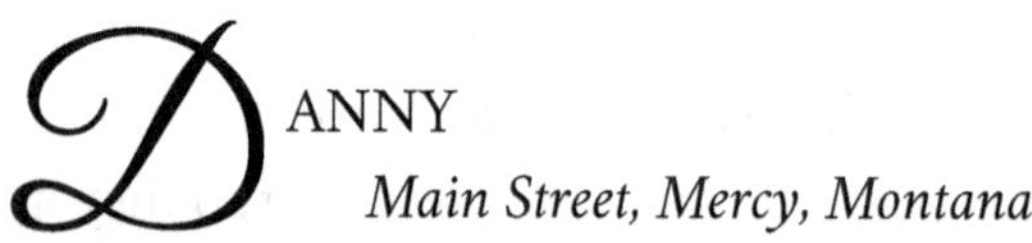

CHAPTER 14

DANNY

Main Street, Mercy, Montana

DANNY HAD no idea what she was getting herself into when she offered to drive the wagon. Her head injury prevented her from doing anything too physical, so it had sounded better than lying on the couch. However, watching the raw meat loaded into the wagon and smelling it the whole way into town was bad enough. Then they had to help unload it and wash the blood out of the back afterward. By the end, she and Chloe had as much blood on them as Tom had.

"Ugh," Chloe gasped as she scrubbed her hands for the third time. "I honestly don't know if I'll be able to eat a steak tomorrow."

They were standing behind the farmers' market, at a hand-washing station that Patty had insisted be set up to help keep the area sanitary. Smoke from the huge smokehouse Caleb had built in the city square was already wafting through the town, and despite everything, Danny's mouth was watering. "I dunno, Chloe," she said, closing her eyes and inhaling deeply. "I've always loved a good steak."

Mercy was bustling with activity as confidence was gradually being restored after the attack. The farmers' market was back in full swing, and Patty had a horde of people setting up tables and decorations for the Fourth of July celebration-slash-barbeque. One of the working generators was out and rumbling away. Valuable fuel was being used to power up a large freezer unit to keep the meat fresh until the next morning. Danny was impressed that someone had gotten a freezer to even work, and assumed it must have been Frankensteined with various parts to achieve it.

"Danny!" Tane called in surprise.

Danny smiled before she even turned around, happy to see her dad. He was on foot and walking fast, not looking nearly as pleased. "What's wrong? Are you okay?"

His step faltered slightly before he stopped in front of them with his hands on his hips. Chuckling, he shook his head at her. "Danny, you're the one who was shot in the head yesterday. And here you are, already being put to work! You're asking me if I'm okay when you're bandaged up and looking like a mummy."

Cringing, Danny reached up absently to pat at the dressing she kept forgetting about. Way to make her feel embarrassed. "I wasn't shot in the *head*, Dad," she corrected while looking around to see if anyone was staring at her. "Stop making it sound so dramatic. It was just my ear." A fresh throbbing in her damaged ear reminded Danny that she needed to stop at the clinic for some Advil.

"Whatever. Your ear is attached to your head. What is she doing out here?" he asked, turning to Chloe. To the girl's credit, Danny noticed she didn't back away from the huge man.

"We just drove the wagon with the meat in it, Mr. Latu,"

Chloe said innocently, failing to mention the physically taxing unloading they'd been roped into. Tom had stayed behind to finish butchering the rest of the cow, and then load it into the second wagon. They thought there'd be more help on the other end.

"Oh! So you're the ones who hijacked my wagon," he said, his grin returning. "That's why I'm here, actually. We're getting further behind on the water by the hour, especially with so many people coming into town tomorrow. They're going to want to fill up before going home. Where's the wagon?"

"City square," Danny said, gesturing to the nearby, large grassy area outside City Hall. "It's already been washed out and is ready to go. Sorry, Dad, we should have brought it back out to you."

Tane raised a meaty hand and waved her off. "Are you kidding? If this means I get to cut into a large chunk of meat tomorrow, I'll work twice as long moving water between now and then."

It was Danny's turn to frown as he walked away.

"What's his meds situation like?" Chloe asked, correctly interpreting Danny's concern.

"Only a couple doses left," Danny replied absently, still watching him as he crossed the street and made his way into the courtyard. She turned thoughtfully to Chloe. "Once the watershed was done being built and the supply train all figured out, it's been primarily handled these past few days by my dad and a handful of other volunteers. I know he doesn't mind, and it's actually a great way to keep him busy. He's always been happiest when he has too much to do, which is one of the reasons he had a heart attack in the first place."

"So, what can I do to help?" Chloe pushed, again accurately reading into Danny's dialogue. She hadn't realized how perceptive the teen was.

Danny grinned at Chloe before draping an arm conspiratorially around her shoulders. She was so much shorter than Danny that it was almost comical. "Patty already corralled me into helping her all morning with the cooking and prep work for the party. Plus, my dad would never accept my help. You heard him!"

Chloe turned her head enough to look up at Danny, but she was smiling and didn't pull away, so Danny continued. "As far as I know, there's only going to be one other gal helping with the water run in the morning. Do you think you—"

"You don't even need to ask," Chloe interrupted. "With the hay getting done today, Ethan and I will be free all morning. We'll both go and make sure your dad doesn't have to do anything except sit and watch."

Relief flooded Danny and she gave Chloe a squeeze. She admired the girl's intelligence, as well as her work ethic. Maybe she'd end up recruiting her for the fire department. She had the right personality for it.

The sound of another wagon jangling down the street reached them, and they both quickly scooted around the back of the booth they were behind. Danny was surprised to see Tom and Bishop so soon, though she certainly wasn't disappointed. Maybe, if they finished unloading fast enough, they could get back to the farm in time to eat dinner together. She'd heard a rumor from Sandy that they would set aside a small amount of meat. Her mouth watered again.

Before anyone could call out a greeting, Sheriff Waters came running up in a hurry, pushing around a couple in the road and causing some inquisitive looks from some bystanders. "Tom! Do you have your radio on?"

Tom yanked the radio off his belt and twisted the dial. "No, the battery was almost dead, so I turned it off during the ride into town. What's up?"

"Sheriff, do you read? What should we do? Over."

The voice squawking over the radios was high-pitched and clearly stressed. Any feeling of contentment Danny had evaporated in an instant. It could be anything, of course, from someone falling off a ladder to an all-out attack, but she knew instinctively that it was something significant.

"Soldiers," Waters said without any preamble. "At the north gate. Not sure how many."

Tom leapt down from the wagon and keyed up the radio. "How many, and what's your situation?" There were a few seconds of silence before he got a response.

"We've got six armed soldiers and a couple of...civilians. Guy named Hicks says Bishop will want to see him."

Danny felt uneasy as Bishop jumped down next to Tom, who was eying him suspiciously. Chloe gasped at the same time and took a step in their direction.

"Hicks is the other counselor!" Chloe exclaimed. "The one who left our hiking group to go find the other kids."

Danny could tell by Bishop's expression that there was a whole lot more going on. He took the radio from Tom's hand without comment and spoke into it. "This is Bishop. Hold your position. Let them know I'm on my way with Mayor Miller and Sheriff Waters."

Tom snatched the radio back from Bishop right as he finished the transmission, his anger barely contained. "You care to fill us in on what we're walking into?"

"Hicks wouldn't lead anyone here if it wasn't safe," Bishop said.

Unsatisfied with the explanation, Tom took a step closer to him. "I want to know who he is, and why the hell he's led a group of soldiers to my town!"

People nearby were beginning to take notice and stopping to listen. Danny cautiously moved in between the two men and set a hand on Tom's arm. "I think we should trust him," she said quietly, glancing around at the onlookers. "We have to trust *someone*, Tom."

"Hicks is a captain in the US Army," Bishop whispered, so that only those closest to him could hear. "I have no idea who's with him, but if he's here, it's important, and we're going to want to at least talk to him."

"I've already got one of my deputies on his way here," Sheriff Waters said. "How about the four of us go see who's knocking?"

"Five," Danny corrected.

"Six," Chloe said, moving closer to Danny. "And don't even try to tell me to go home," she added, before Tom or Bishop could give her the order. "I know Hicks. He was kind of a jerk, but I don't think he'd hurt anyone."

Bishop scoffed, and everyone visibly relaxed slightly, including Danny. "Chloe's right on both counts," he confirmed.

Tom still looked irritated, but he reclipped his radio and gestured up the road with his head. "All right. I don't see that we have much of a choice. Let's go."

Danny smiled reassuringly to the couple of people lingering near them, and she didn't notice anyone following as they walked together up Main Street. Her stomach was in knots, and didn't improve after the sheriff's deputy joined them with an additional rifle. Since Tom and Bishop already had theirs, she took the extra. However, if there were really soldiers at the gate, Danny doubted any of their weapons would do much compared to automatic rifles.

It didn't take long to travel the mile to where the road was barricaded at the northern end of Mercy. The buildings thinned out fast and what houses lined the street were spread out over several-acre lots. The roadblock was closer there than the one to the south, as the north road didn't lead directly to any other towns. It was very rarely used by anyone trying to gain entry into Mercy.

As they approached it, Danny could see what looked like a rather large group of men gathered, most of them in camo gear, and all heavily armed. One was wearing outdoor clothing and standing next to an attractive, middle-aged woman. A particular soldier stood out from the rest due to his dauting size. He was incredibly tall, and built like a bull. There was something vaguely familiar about him, but Danny couldn't remember from where or why.

Bishop's pace suddenly quickened until he was almost running, leaving the rest of them behind to scramble to keep up. "Stay here," Tom directed to Danny and Chloe as he unslung his rifle and ran after him. From the look on Tom's face, she guessed he recognized the soldier, too.

Before Danny could decide what to do, Bishop stopped ten feet from the gate. He had his back to her, but she could see the reaction from the huge soldier, as his shoulders sagged and he pushed past the fencing without even acknowledging the startled guards.

Tom and Sheriff Waters stared in bewilderment at the two men, but didn't try to interfere as they approached each other.

Danny watched in stunned silence as the soldier reached out and grasped Bishop by the arms, a huge smile spreading across his handsome face as he spoke. "Hey, Dad."

CHAPTER 15

*J*AMES
    Master Sergeant, US Marines, 1ˢᵗ Force Reconnaissance
Mercy, Montana

JAMES HAD NEVER SEEN his dad so emotional, except for the day they buried his mother. While he had the benefit of knowing his father was going to be in Mercy, the last time they'd spoken, James was about to leave for Germany with his team. Up until that moment, his dad probably thought he was dead.

There was a heavy pause as everyone else became bystanders to their reunion, and it didn't matter to James whether they understood or not. After a long embrace, Bishop stood back and held him at arm's length. "I didn't know you were alive. I thought—"

"The mission got scrubbed," James answered as his dad got too choked up to finish the sentence. "It was a last-minute call, so we were still on base at Malmstrom when the gamma-ray hit."

"Allison and the baby?"

"They were at home at Base Pendleton," James assured his dad about his wife and daughter. "I'd just spoken to Ally before we lost power. I haven't seen or talked to her since, but I've gotten confirmation they're okay." The reality was that James lay awake each night worrying about his family, and would continue to until they were reunited.

Bishop let go of him and seemed to remember suddenly that there were other people there. "Um, Tom, this is my...son. Master Sergeant James Campbell, leader of the 1st Force Reconnaissance."

James shifted his attention to the large man standing behind his father and had an intense feeling of deja vu. He could see the recognition on Tom's face as the woman next to him started to point. "We've met you before," she said, confirming his suspicions.

"What?" Bishop demanded, turning to her. "How?"

"Your son already saved our skins once, back at FEMA Shelter M3," Tom explained, stepping forward to hold out a hand to him. "Nice to see you again. I don't think you ever really met Danny. And this is Sheriff Waters, and Chloe."

"Hey, Hicks," Chloe quipped with a small wave and crooked grin.

James grunted as it all fell into place and he took the hand that Tom offered. He looked different out of the black FEMA gear, and his face had healed, but James still recognized him. His initial assessment of the rancher back at the shelter seemed to have been accurate. Tom was both a fighter and a survivor, and James wasn't surprised to run into him again. And he finally knew where he'd heard the name Mercy before. It had been bugging him for the past two days, as they'd gotten closer to the town.

Bishop was looking back and forth between the three of them

as they became reacquainted. "I don't understand," he said, running a hand over the top of his head in frustration. "What were you doing at the FEMA shelter, James? Where have you been? You were so close this whole time, and I had no idea."

James looked over at his five men before gesturing to the senator. He might as well dump it all on them at once. "First, let's get the introductions out of the way," he said with a forced grin. "I should probably start with US Senator Alicia Jenson. We're doing our best to keep her safe from some rogue military actions. I was hoping Mercy would be a safe refuge."

"It's a pleasure to meet all of you," the senator said as they exchanged pleasantries amid an appropriate amount of shock and confusion. "I get the feeling everyone has long stories to tell and we've been walking for almost two days. Is there a place we can sit down to do it? Preferably over a glass of something with a really high alcohol content."

"Oh, you and my mom are going to get along famously," Tom scoffed. "It sounds like we're having some similar problems." He pointed back over his shoulder. "I think we should all go back to the ranch. We can avoid going through town and there's enough room for everyone."

"Why do we need to avoid the town?" Jay asked, moving up alongside James while giving him a cautionary look.

The sheriff shouldered his rifle and appeared slightly chagrined. "People are a little spooked right now around anyone in a uniform. We'd do best to avoid drawing too much attention until we get a chance to announce your appearance, or else find you something else to wear."

"And there's also a quarantine for any newcomers," Danny said while absently touching her face. James wondered what in the world had happened to her head. It was swathed with a thick layer of bandages and he could see some bruising extending down from under it on her right cheek. If he remembered correctly, the last time he saw her she'd just been racked in the forehead with an AR by a Marine with a bad attitude.

"Quarantine?" Senator Jenson asked with some concern. "Are we at risk of being exposed to something nasty?"

"No," Tom assured them. "It's to protect the town. There was an outbreak before we got here that was caused by some travelers, but there haven't been any new cases for around two weeks."

"I think I've probably heard of it," the senator said, nodding her head. "Something resembling cholera? There were reports of a serious epidemic in Helena, though there aren't any cases in Idaho yet."

"You're the senator of Idaho?" Danny asked, her curiosity clearly deepening.

Before anyone could offer any more information, both of the radios Tom and Sheriff Waters had with them began squawking. James watched as a look passed between them, and then Bishop raised his eyebrows at Tom.

"Okay," Tom said to the unasked question, apparently coming to a decision and making it clear who called the shots. "We're a code four here at the north gate," he said into the radio while looking at James and then the rest of his team, who were all standing at ease behind him. "False alarm."

"Mayor?" one of the guards asked, looking somewhat uncomfortable. "What do you want us to tell people?"

"The truth," Tom said pointedly. "We're not attempting to cover anything up here, John. If anyone wants to know, we've had a member of the US civilian government and her escort arrive, asking for shelter. The sheriff and I are taking them to the farm and we'll make an official announcement about our guests tomorrow at the barbeque."

James noted how all three guards were visibly reassured by Tom's direct approach, and his respect for the man as a leader deepened. It was a smart move. It also reminded him that they had an audience, and he didn't want to have the upcoming conversation where anyone else could overhear.

"Let's get moving," Tom directed, mirroring James' thoughts. He pulled the barricade open wider. "It's several miles to my ranch."

"I'll send my deputy back to get the wagon," Sheriff Waters offered, while gesturing to the man in question who had been standing quietly off to the side the whole time. "No need to say anything specific, Jim. Just get it emptied and explain that you're taking it back to the ranch."

"You got it, Sheriff," Jim answered eagerly, already walking away with a wave. "I'll catch up to ya as fast as I can!"

"Did you walk all the way here from the Trek Thru Trouble office?" Chloe asked as they began walking, looking pointedly at Hicks. "Why didn't you come sooner, if you knew we were here?"

"We came part of the way on a helicopter," Jay answered. "Our recon unit just got to the office a couple of days ago."

"It's complicated," Hicks said, without further explanation.

Senator Jenson moved next to Bishop, and James groaned when he saw the look on her face. "I'm not sure who outranks whom here, but I'm guessing that you might be the man I need to direct my questions to. I'm hoping you have the authority to fill us all in on what it is we're doing out here." The senator spread her arms wide and waved them around at the surrounding mountains and endless trees. "Because I still have no idea why I'm out in the middle of nowhere."

His dad turned from the woman who was used to getting her way and stared at James. She watched the exchange and rolled her eyes. "Look, General Montgomery essentially put out a hit on me, and your son and his team decided to disobey orders and whisked me away, instead. I appreciate what they've done for me, but I'm in the dark as to why I've been brought here. I'm not buying the excuse that it's simply a good place to hide. I need details, especially if I'm going to help with whatever it is you guys are in the middle of. The civilian government and military need to work together, with the people, if we have any shot of making it through this."

"She's definitely right about that," Danny agreed. "Coming from someone who's been caught in the middle, if Senator Jenson has a shot at bridging the gap, now would be a good time to start talking, Bishop."

James knew just from his dad's body posture that he was resigned to exposing everything, and he gave Jay a look. He hadn't shared the truth of the vault with his team, though they had to know something more was at stake when he'd ordered Corporal Lance to stay back with Hawk. While the two men could never hold off a direct military assault, James didn't want to leave the kids completely defenseless in the unlikely event that some other rogue group attacked them. At the time, he still thought the office would be safer for the teens than the trip to Mercy.

"The Trek Thru Trouble program and office is a cover for the largest and most sophisticated seed vault in the world," Bishop said. "There are three of them in the US, but Trek's is the main one. I was part of the team that designed and built it, and I've been in charge of protecting it since it went operational a year ago."

"Seed vault?" Senator Jenson asked. It was the first time James had seen her at a loss for words. "As in, there's a storage facility under that building?"

"A massive structure," Hicks confirmed. "It's tied into a pre-existing cave system, and it's not just a seed vault. They're genetically modified seeds and animal embryos, stored in self-germinating containers in a nuclear and EMP-hardened infrastructure. Just the two vaults located here and in Oregon are more than enough to enable what's left of our population to be self-sustaining in harsher environments than what we're already facing."

Danny was shaking her head. "This doesn't make sense. What does this have to do with some general trying to kill a senator, or Mercy?"

"Have you heard of General Montgomery?" James asked. "The Four-star general left in charge of the military?"

Tom nodded. "We heard bits and pieces about the general when we were in the shelter, and Caleb's interpreted and put together some of the military's infrastructure based on the transmissions he's picked up."

"The general has been using my unit as his personal SWAT team," James explained. "Did you know you were on the Survivor List?" he asked his dad.

Bishop frowned and turned to him thoughtfully. "I was notified, but at the time never thought it would be activated. Even now, while I was staying hidden in order to protect The Farm, I didn't think the list would come into play. It's stored at Mount Weather."

James raised his eyebrows and then put out a hand to stop his dad's next question. "Later," he promised. "General Montgomery was using it as a means to gather the people he needed to get control of the vault. He's a smart guy and he saw where the power was going to be several moves ahead of anyone else."

"If your job was to protect the vault, why wouldn't you immediately hand it over to the military?" Chloe asked, and James was surprised she was the first one to ask the question. "Isn't that who you work for, Bishop?" There was a cutting edge to her words.

They had followed Tom onto the first side road, which was already heading up a wooded hill, and they were clear of any houses at the moment. Bishop stopped in the middle of the road so he could address the whole group and James watched his dad with a strange sense of detachment. It was as if the whole situation was too surreal to be happening.

"When I first got to Mercy, the kids were still my first priority, and then finding out the full extent of what had happened," Bishop said, glancing at Chloe. "By the time I was ready to make my way back to my post at The Farm, I got the second radio working and discovered Hicks was already there. At that point, we were getting word of the civilian attacks carried out by the military. Hicks had reports of unrest among several different factions, so we decided it would be in the nation's best interest to sit on The Farm until we knew who was going to end up in power."

"I think that was the right move." Senator Jenson was the first to speak, and James wasn't expecting her reaction. "These vaults are incredibly valuable. We can't let them become part of a power struggle or else we might end up losing everything. Montgomery has to be stopped. He'll use it as a way to maintain control over the population and would literally have the ability to choose who lives and dies. No one man should ever have that authority."

The sound of horses approaching at a gallop caused the whole group to turn and look up the road. Both Lucas and Jay began to bring their ARs around until James waved them off. The last thing they needed was to get into an unwarranted shootout with a local.

"Ethan!" Tom shouted as two riders came into view. One of them was the same young man James met at the shelter, who he remembered was Tom's son. The boy had been reaching for a rifle kept in a scabbard on his saddle. James assumed it was normally used for hunting, but it was obvious the teen had no qualms about facing off against any potential threat.

"We heard the exchange on the radio," the other rider answered. He was a large, muscular Hispanic man, and was holding a radio.

"We're okay, Chief," Danny offered, and then looked at Ethan as he pulled up on an impressive black-and-white horse. "But we appreciate the gesture."

"Whoa!" Ethan exclaimed while pointing at James. "You're the dude who took care of Dillinger for us." He looked at the five other uniformed, armed soldiers, and his smile faltered as he shifted in his saddle to face his dad.

"We're good here," Tom confirmed. "We're all headed to the ranch. It would be better if we hold off on explaining everything until then."

Ethan smiled again and looked down at Chloe. "Want a ride?" The young girl reached up and he easily pulled her into the saddle with him. The horse turned in a circle as the teen first gestured to James, and then addressed the rest of the group. He said the one thing that could unequivocally bring them all together in that moment. "When was the last time any of you had a good steak?"

As he watched the reaction of his men, and the camaraderie that was already expanding, it began to make sense to James. How his dad and Tom were already connected to each other, and to Mercy. They had all been on a collision course without knowing it.

"Call it fate, or whatever you want, but we're obviously all here for a reason," James said. He looked around at the unusual collection of people in the middle of a country road already being reclaimed by nature. "Let's not waste it."

CHAPTER 16

Miller Ranch, Mercy, Montana

THE UNPLANNED DINNER included their large group of sixteen, as well as Tom's mom, Sam, and the other nine volunteers Chief Martinez was a part of. They used up most of the beef he'd set aside, though it was more than worth it. After everyone seemed to accept the explanation that the senator and her entourage were seeking refuge after their helicopter ran out of gas, there was nothing but good cheer and laughter. Tom used his pull as mayor to waive the quarantine protocol, claiming their two-day isolation during their hike was acceptable since they hadn't encountered anyone else.

The sheriff and his deputy took the volunteers back to town in the wagon as soon as they were done eating. It gave Tom the opportunity to catch his mom and Sam up on some details before making plans for the night, with the promise of a thorough conversation once everyone was settled.

"Tom, do you copy?"

Tom winced before unhooking the radio from his belt. By then, Sheriff Waters would have stopped and had a long conversation with Patty at City hall, where she would be preparing most of the night for the celebration the next day. She'd already radioed them several times for more information and he knew she wasn't going to be satisfied with what the sheriff told her.

"Go ahead, Patty," he said into the radio without any enthusiasm. He just hoped she'd remember that there were several other people listening to them.

"Sheriff Waters just left. I'll see you when you get here bright and early tomorrow and we'll have a nice, long talk. I have a few questions for you."

"I'm sure you do," he muttered, before keying up the radio. "Received." He figured it was best not to give any existing gossip more fuel than necessary, so he held off on saying anything else. However, he'd be sure to remind Patty in the morning that she was the one who basically forced him into the Mayor position.

"Thanks for the tents," James said as he approached with two bottles of beer in his hands.

Tom was happy for the distraction, and took one of the bottles. He'd been busy working on getting a fire going in the backyard fire pit. It was already getting dark and the temperature was quickly dropping, plus it always seemed the best conversations were held over a campfire.

"No problem. If you end up needing more sleeping bags or anything else, all the camping gear is stored in the same place as the tents, in the barn."

James gave a nod, picked up an ax, and began chopping wood from a nearby pile. He easily split the pieces with a one-handed swing, while drinking the beer. His men were all in the field behind the barn, setting up a couple of tents for them to stay in. It was the best form of security Tom could have, so when the three volunteers showed up after dinner to stand guard, he'd sent them home.

Grace ran up and licked at his face as Tom bent down to blow on the flame he'd started. Laughing, he looked around for Danny. The dog's appearance was a sure sign that she was close by.

Sure enough, she was just stepping off the back porch and headed their way, a fresh, smaller bandage on her head. "Is it story time yet?" she asked, looking at both Tom and James. His mom and Sam were with her, looking a little apprehensive. "Bishop went to find Ethan and Chloe," Danny explained. "I guess Crissy is going to stay in town tonight to help Patty."

Tom patted a stump near him for her to sit down, and then gestured at the box full of bottles that Sam was carrying. "You found my stash?" he teased.

"I put these in the creek earlier. I didn't think you'd mind," Sam answered, setting the box down with a rattle of glass. Removing one, he raised it toward James. "I expect full disclosure now."

James dropped the ax and approached the fire, exchanging his empty bottle for a fresh one. "You were already going to get it," he promised. He pivoted toward Tom, looking even more intimidating in the growing firelight. "I told my men to dig in for the night, and we'll be patrolling the area near the main field and trail."

"I appreciate that," Tom said, feeling more at ease than he had in a long time. Even though he knew there was a looming threat from Dillinger and perhaps the military itself, he finally felt like enough of the pieces of the puzzle were coming together. With all of them working on it, maybe they could get a clear view of what they were up against.

"Where's the senator?" James asked, addressing Sandy. "She needs to be a part of this conversation."

Sandy chose a stump in between Danny and Sam and then

waved a hand towards the house behind them. "I got her settled into the girls' room and she said something about making herself feel human again before meeting us out here in a few minutes. My guess is that involves both the clean clothes and bottle of wine I gave her."

Tom chuckled and tossed another log on the fire, building it up until it provided plenty of light around the firepit. Just as he figured, Senator Jenson and his mom had hit it off immediately.

Lightning flickered to the east, though it was silent, which only made it more eerie. The alternating hot days and cold nights followed by bizarre storms was beginning to at least become a little predictable. Of course, as soon as Tom thought he had it figured out, it was bound to change again.

Tom saw James stiffen before he even heard the footsteps approaching, and he looked away from the sky to see Hicks and Bishop leading Ethan and Chloe over from the barn. Tom chose to assume that they were covered in hay because they'd been working on stacking the last of the bales. Still, he'd have a talk with Ethan later, just to make sure.

As they all got situated, Senator Jenson finally joined them, shooing Sam over so she could sit next to his mom. She appeared very sober and cleaner in the borrowed clothes. "Let's get this party started," the senator said as she sat down, rubbing her hands together with enthusiasm. Sandy offered her a beer, but she shook her head. "Thanks, but only water for me the rest of the night. I've decided I need to be clearheaded for this."

The fire snapped and flared between them as they all listened in rapt fascination while James described Cheyenne Mountain, Mount Weather, and the various missions ordered by General Montgomery. Although James explained the Survivor List, and Bishop gave more details on the seed vault, Tom still had plenty of questions. He could feel things speeding up and that Senator Jenson and James were now inexplicably a part of their journey.

While Tom had always suspected Bishop was withholding things, he was shocked to discover who the man really was and what he was involved in. It was hard for Tom to reconcile his feelings toward him. While Bishop had been a huge help to both the farm and town, the look on his mom's face made it difficult for him to be too appreciative. She obviously didn't know and had to be struggling with her own emotions. The only reason Tom didn't take his chances with the guy in another attempt to throw him out was because he believed Bishop when he said he was only doing what he thought was best for everyone involved. However, it was clear that the vault and their ability to access it was both a blessing and a curse.

"How did this general know about the seed vault?" Sam asked. He was understandably ecstatic when he first found out about the seeds, but was smart enough to quickly grasp the danger of it.

"He was part of the initial review board for the project," Bishop explained. "After it was approved, his involvement was over, which is why he doesn't know where they are. Nearly everyone involved was kept blind to every other aspect of it, other than what their specific assignment was."

"Do you know a Dr. Watson?" James asked.

Bishop's head snapped up and he looked at his son with enough apprehension that Tom leaned forward to hear the answer. "How do you know that name?"

James frowned at his dad. "She was the first asset from the Survivor List we recovered."

Bishop stood and stared out at the deepening darkness, his concern palpable. "She's at Cheyenne Mountain with General Montgomery?"

"Last I heard. What's the matter, Dad?" James stood with him and crossed his arms over his chest, reminding Tom of a grizzly bear.

Shaking his head as if to rid himself of something, Bishop sat back down and gestured for James to do the same. "I might have been naïve to think I could keep the vault hidden. Dr. Watson was the lead geneticist on the project. We met several times, to go over the specs on the storage designs. She was never directly on-site, but the woman is smart. It wouldn't be hard for her to figure out, geographically, the region the three vaults are in."

"There's not a whole lot out here," James replied.

"And Mercy is already on their radar," Tom said, feeling his unease growing.

"Can they get inside?" Danny asked. "I mean, if they find the vault. How hard is it to get in?"

"It can withstand a direct hit from a nuke, and there are only a handful of people with access," Bishop said, looking again at James. "The president and top twelve successors, who are currently all presumed dead. Otherwise, just myself, two other top officials who are also likely gone…and James."

"Yeah," James said with some sarcasm directed at Hicks. "I already found out about that. It's some science fiction-like contraption you have to breathe on."

"Cool," Chloe said, speaking for the first time. Other than glaring at Bishop, Tom hadn't heard her say much the whole afternoon.

"James was my failsafe," Bishop said, spreading his hands. "I knew that if anything were to happen, if anyone could track me or this project down, it would be him."

"I'd say you were right," Hicks said.

"So, where do we go from here?" Senator Jenson asked, interrupting the growing tension. "What's done is done, and at this point we have no control over General Montgomery and what he does or doesn't know. The reality is that if Montgomery has the backing of the joint commanders behind him, I don't even know if my reinstating a civilian government will have any effect."

"Is that a possibility?" Sandy asked, her eyes wide.

"I'm working on it," Jenson answered with a wink.

Tom's eyes narrowed as he studied the politician with a new perspective. There might still be more questions than answers, but some things were definitely becoming clearer to him. "So we keep you safe until that has a chance to play out."

James shifted on his stump to face Tom and made a grunting noise, which he took as a sign of agreement. "We also need to keep you two alive," Tom added, gesturing to both James and Bishop. "That's why the access was designed that way, right? You have to be alive to breathe on it."

Bishop smiled then. "Yes, it was, and that is one aspect of the project that Montgomery is also aware of."

"That gives us a strong bargaining chip," Hicks stated. "I mean, if it comes down to that, we let Montgomery know where you are, Bishop. He can't risk doing anything that could kill you, and he doesn't know James has access."

James turned and gave Hicks a look that made Tom smile. It was obvious the two men didn't get along, but he thought the huge man was about to hug Hicks. The idea that they had an upper hand with something so valuable gave them the opportunity to move from being completely defensive, to the ones making the demands. If they handled things right, it might be just what the senator needed to shift the power.

Danny leaned into him then, and held tightly to his arm. "It helps knowing that it was worth it."

Turning, he wrapped his arms around her, not caring what sort of comments or questions it might provoke from the others. "What do you mean?" he asked, her thick black hair soft against his cheek.

Tilting her head up, she pulled back enough to see his face. "That everything we went through, Tom, especially at the FEMA shelter, was for a reason. This isn't just about Mercy anymore."

As Danny rested her forehead against his chest, Tom felt the bandages and was reminded again of how close he'd come to losing everything. Was it all worth it? He saw Bishop staring at them through the dancing firelight. His son, against all odds, seated next to him.

Tom agreed with what James had said earlier that day. It was more than a coincidence their paths had already crossed in so many ways. And while Danny was also right that it was becoming bigger than them all, it seemed that first, everything was converging on Mercy.

CHAPTER 17

Chloe

Miller Ranch, Mercy, Montana

Chloe kicked at a crooked bale of hay and instantly regretted it as pain shot through her foot. There were only a few of the awkward bundles left to organize, but since Ethan's dad pulled him aside for a "talk" when they were leaving the bonfire, she decided to finish the work on her own. Chloe had made a promise to Danny to help Tane with the water the next day, so she planned on having the chore totally done that night so they wouldn't have to mess with it before leaving in the morning.

Everyone else was committed to being at the barbeque setup at the crack of dawn. Even the new arrivals were going in to meet with Patty and the other council members. Tom said something about clearing the air before the festivities, but Chloe really couldn't care less. She wasn't in much of a mood for a party anymore.

Why everything in her life had to continuously get turned

upside-down just when she was getting used to it, she couldn't understand. Was it too much to hope for more than two days without some new revelation or confrontation?

"You're still working on that hay?"

Chloe froze at the sound of Bishop's voice and didn't turn around. "Someone has to," she muttered, kicking the bale again despite the fresh flare of discomfort. He was the last person she wanted to talk to.

When she heard Bishop approaching and saw him reach for the last bale on the ground, she turned on him. "I don't need your help!" she yelled, yanking the grass from his hands, only to drop it. "Just go up to your secret lair and play with your radio."

"Chloe—"

"No!" she wailed, startling herself with the anger suddenly coursing through her. "You don't get to apologize. Not now. Not when the *only* reason you finally told the truth is because you had to."

"The truth?" Bishop countered. "You do understand what we're talking about here, right? Because I know how smart you are, so don't play stupid with me."

He wasn't intimidated by her rage the way most people were, and that only made Chloe more furious. "You never cared about us!" she spat. "You don't care about *any* of us. We were just a cover. I'm sure you couldn't wait to get rid of us."

Bishop frowned. "You don't really believe that."

Chloe took a step back, bumping into the haystack, and put a hand out to steady herself. Thinking back over the first part of the Trek Thru Trouble hike, her face flushed with humiliation at the understanding that none of them were even counselors. That the poor lost souls they were dragging through the mountains were nothing more than a means to an end. Chloe's shame deepened with the acknowledgement that she'd actually started to fall for their charade, and remembered what Ripley had whispered to her right before she'd left for Helena. That things weren't what they seemed.

Scoffing, Chloe pushed away from the stacks of straw and staggered past Bishop. "Ripley was a part of this too, wasn't she?" It was more an accusation than a question and Bishop's only response was to briefly look away from her. "Well, at least she decided her family was more important than her *duty*."

A flash of anger flickered across Bishop's face and his hands clenched into fists, giving Chloe a brief feeling of satisfaction. "That's not fair, Chloe. I thought my son was dead, and my daughter-in-law and grandchild were well beyond my reach."

"Fair?" Chloe made an odd sound between a laugh and a sob. "My parents probably *are* dead, Bishop. You were supposed to be helping me find them! You made me believe you cared about me! I don't have any—" A real sob escaped her then, and she clamped a hand over her mouth to smother it.

Bishop was wise enough to not approach her, and instead raised both hands out to her. "You're right. It was an assignment, but that doesn't mean the relationships we built weren't real."

Chloe looked away. She wanted to believe him. She knew Ethan and Crissy were her friends, and that if she could get herself to think rationally about it, she wasn't alone. It was just that Bishop had been her one steady port in the storm. Chloe realized, standing there feeling like a part of her was being ripped out, that she'd come to think of Bishop as a father figure. The one person she could trust. The deep betrayal she was experiencing extended beyond the counselor façade and into something that represented so much more.

"My own son grew up never knowing what his dad really did," Bishop said gently. "My wife died in a car accident while I was overseas on an assignment she knew nothing about. James had to identify her body by himself because I wasn't there. He was seventeen."

Chloe's resolve faltered and she pivoted slowly to face him. She saw the same man she'd had meaningful conversations with for the past month. The raw pain on his normally neutral face made it hard to maintain her resentment, but the ugliness in Chloe that she fought so hard to control wouldn't be denied. "Is the fact that you did the same thing to your own family supposed to make it okay?"

Bishop flinched, and the familiar feeling of shame came quick on the heels of Chloe's fury. "I'm sorry," she gasped, finding it hard to breathe. All of the fight suddenly left her, and Chloe struggled to pull herself out of the darkness of her own mind. She turned to flee, to attempt to run from herself the way she always had before, but strong arms wrapped her up from behind, preventing her escape.

"Not this time, Chloe," Bishop whispered, close to her ear. "I care too much about you to let you go. We're in this together for the long haul, kid, so kick me, hit me, bite me. Do whatever it is you need to do to get it off your chest, but I'm not letting you go."

Sagging, Chloe tried desperately to tap back into her rage. To retreat into the comfort of the numbness it offered. It was so much easier. It didn't hurt nearly as much. Instead, she turned around and allowed Bishop to hug her as she sobbed. She cried for her mom, for her dad, and all the other people in her life she might never see again. As the tears finally began to subside, Chloe realized that Bishop was still there. He really wasn't going to leave...and she began to believe that maybe it *would* be okay.

*E*MILY

Banff National Park, Alberta, Canada

EMILY WAS ALMOST certain she was dying.

The tent flap billowed gently in the soft morning breeze, a paradox for what it was hiding inside. Emily watched it move, mesmerized by the fluttering motion and the odd sound of a local bird. What had her father called it? A bitter, or something like that. It made this weird dripping sound followed by a whoop that reminded her of a plunger. Just as Emily started to drift off again, it startled her awake, making her think someone was approaching her through the marshy field nearby until she realized it was only the bird.

Her dad never came back. He promised he would, after finding her mom and younger brother at the nearby town. They had gone there the morning of the power outage to get some more ice and hot dogs. Hot dogs.

Emily's mouth watered despite her severe dehydration,

forcing her to stick her swollen tongue partway out of her mouth so she could smack her lips and swallow painfully. She hadn't eaten for over a week. Maybe two.

The nineteen-year-old girl had always considered herself to be strong and independent. Normally, that was true, but Emily had fallen apart over the past ten days. She'd been doing all right up until the first big storm. After finally catching a fish, the torrential rain flooded her fire so she was forced to eat it raw. She wasn't desperate enough then to eat the whole thing. Now? She would have happily slurped down the eyeballs and innards that she'd stupidly tossed aside.

Camping in Banff National Park was a summer trip her mom had wanted to take for years. When her dad announced he could get the two weeks off from work that year, they'd spent hours planning all the details. Emily's fifteen-year-old brother was just as excited, and he and her dad got new fishing poles as well as the tent. Emily was less than enthused, as she had what she liked to call real-life problems since graduating from high school and entering the harsh world of college. It was only under the threat of being disowned that she finally caved and agreed to go. Her mom would have never done it, but—

Emily blinked slowly as her thoughts muddied and she forgot where she was. When the dusky interior of the tent came back into focus, replacing the safety of the family room, she made a small whimpering sound. She wasn't home. She would never be home again. She was alone in the tent in a remote campground in the middle of nowhere and no one was coming to help her.

Using the surge of panic to lend her strength, Emily reached out, determined to drag herself outside. Horror quickly mixed in with her other rising emotions as she realized she could barely lift her arm. Her eyes wide, Emily searched for the water bottle and saw it lying a few inches away, empty. She remembered then, sucking down the last few drops sometime during the long night. When was the last time she'd gone to pee?

It was a mistake to stay in the tent. If someone wandered by, they would assume the campground was abandoned. Although it was a remote site, there had been a few other campers near the lake when they first arrived. That was one of the reasons her father had her stay there when he decided to go find the rest of their family. He thought it would be safer for Emily at the campground than in town, since they had no idea what would be going on there.

The first week hadn't been so bad, aside from the unbearable weight of not knowing what had happened to everyone. Several times, Emily had taken her backpack and started down the gravel road, determined to go find them herself. However, each time she ended up panicking after going for miles without seeing another person, until she finally turned around. The farther she got from the false safety of the tent, the more intense her fear became, until she couldn't overcome it. The nearest town was more than forty miles away and Emily had no way of knowing what she might encounter on the way. Besides, back then, she still had some food left and plenty of water. The fire was going and she was confident she could get by for weeks, if she had to.

By the time Emily realized her mistake, she was too weak to leave and the other campers had disappeared the first few days after the event. She was alone. She would die alone.

Normally, as soon as the sun came out the tent would start to warm up, but it was different that morning. Emily shivered uncontrollably and she suspected her body had lost the ability to regulate its temperature. That was something she'd learned about in one of her pre-nursing classes.

A tear slid down her cheek, the precious fluid cutting a trail through the dirt before soaking into the pillowcase. Her vision blurring, Emily once again thought she might have been lying in her bed at home, and she clung to the illusion that time. Was that her mom lying next to her?

With the last of her strength, Emily balled her mother's favorite sweatshirt in her hand, forgetting how she had pulled it over her head the night before to help block out the cold. "Mommy..." she whispered into the fabric, taking a shuddering breath. "I'll be home soon."

CHAPTER 19

PATTY

City Center, Mercy, Montana

"HERE, USE THIS ONE, SERGEANT—" Patty hesitated in front of the homemade brick grill, trying to remember the soldier's name.

"You can just call me Jay," the young man said with a grin. "And while I'm happy to help you out, I can't guarantee any of the steaks I cook will be edible."

Patty waved off his concern before handing Jay a lighter. After the last town dinner, they'd swapped out the metal barbeques for the much larger wood-burning grills. She was rather proud of the craftsmanship, and they should last for years to come. "I have a feeling there won't be too many critics here today."

They'd just finished an early-morning meeting with the city leaders, where they'd all unanimously welcomed Senator Jenson and the 1st Force Recon Unit. Patty had a private talk with Tom beforehand where he filled her in on the seed vault, a detail omitted from the rest of the council members. She understood the need to withhold the information for the time being, but it was a good reminder of why she stepped down in the first place. Patty was in her element ordering everyone around in the town square. She was happy to leave the political maneuverings and life-or-death decisions to Tom.

"Patty!" Melissa walked across the square with way too much purpose for the early hour.

Patty knew the doctor missed the meeting due to some sort of medical emergency, though she hadn't gotten any details. "Is everything okay?"

Melissa nodded, a large smile spreading across her face. "Yes! Carrie delivered a healthy baby girl a couple of hours ago."

Her chest swelling with joy, Patty hugged Melissa and then clapped her hands together. "Something else to celebrate today!"

"I'm picking up a few things for Carrie from the clinic, but I should be back in time for the food," Melissa explained, already walking backwards. "I'll see you later!"

Her step lighter, Patty made her way across the stage and towards the other cooking area that was basically in the alley behind City Hall. She needed to make sure the two soldiers had found the tasks she'd assigned them, which was overseeing boiling corn, potatoes, and eggs. The rest of the 1st Force Recon team were on an extra water-run to the river. Patty didn't want to use the purified spring water for cooking.

It was going to take large amounts of water to boil all the food necessary to feed upwards of five hundred people. They expected a good turnout for the Fourth of July celebration, and not only because of the promised meat. It was close to a month since the gamma-ray burst changed all of their lives, and their emotional needs were now becoming just as important as their physical. Patty knew they could throw as much food and comfort as possible at the people of Mercy, but without the proper sense of community and hope, none of that would matter. Especially with the threat of a military takeover looming. A defeated town might welcome the intrusion.

That was where Patty saw herself as most valuable, aside from helping with the medical needs at the clinic. She would do her best to work as the glue that helped hold the community spirit together. Patty had lived in Mercy for most of her life and loved the town and the people in it. The complete isolation they'd been forced into was something they needed to embrace and learn to cope with, and she knew the best way to do that was to focus on the people who remained. Together, they could accomplish whatever needed to be done, but only if they didn't lose sight of what it was that made them call Mercy home in the first place.

"Riders!"

Patty had been staring at her feet as she walked while reminiscing, and she jerked to a stop at the shout from the soldier she'd been approaching. He was pointing down the alley, and sure enough, there were two riders charging up the side street.

Tom appeared from behind her and he paused long enough to fill her in. "It's the returning Pony Express riders we sent to check out the station. South gate radioed they were on their way in with some news."

As they neared, it was obvious to Patty that the news wasn't good. They looked utterly exhausted, dirty, and their horses were spent.

"The station is gone," one of them shouted without any preamble, and Patty realized the filthy man was their main rider, Jed. "Taken over by a bunch of soldiers."

Tom exchanged a look with Bishop, who had followed him into the alley. "Were you able to learn anything about who they are or what they're doing?" Tom asked. He held the horse steady while the man slid to the ground, barely able to stand on his own.

"No," Jed said apologetically. "I'll be honest with ya, Tom.

Those guys scared the crap outta me. Had to be at least a couple dozen, all armed and with horses. They meant business and I have a family to take care of."

"It's okay, Jed," Tom said, placing a hand on the other man's shoulder. "I wouldn't want you to take any extra risks. We all appreciate you bringing back this news, though. Now we know who Caleb is really talking to," he added, turning to Bishop.

Patty watched the conversation with a growing sense of unease. It was safe to assume Dillinger was behind the attack on the station. Not only was he getting closer to Mercy, but he'd effectively cut off their supply train. The medication and other first aid provisions were already dangerously low. Without the ability to scavenge or trade for more, they were going to be vulnerable to various medical issues and the subsequent deaths, for those with conditions requiring treatment.

"It looked like they were getting ready for something though," the other rider added, still on her mount. "Horses were being packed up and they even had a wagon out with a bunch of supplies in it. We rode hard for two days to get word back to you." The woman glanced around at the group in the alley, and then the row of large pots cooking over the open fires. "You still doing the barbeque thing today? I'm assuming you made it back in time to stop those outlaws?"

Patty realized the riders had no idea what had transpired over the past three days and were likely half-starved and sleep-deprived. Looking around, she spotted Crissy pushing Trevor in a wheelchair. "Crissy!" she called, waving the girl over. "Take these two and find them some food."

Crissy turned in their direction, laboring to get Trevor across the long grass. "Sure thing, so long as we can eat too?"

"Sure," Patty agreed absently as she stared at Trevor. The teen with his splinted leg sticking out reminded her that Russell had never showed at the clinic the day before and she hadn't seen him anywhere that morning. "Crissy, was Father Rogers at the clinic when you left?"

Crissy shrugged. "I haven't seen him in a couple of days, maybe three. Why?"

Patty's brows creased as she shook her head. "Never mind. It doesn't matter how he chooses to spend his time. Thank you for helping."

"We'll take care of the horses," Tom assured the riders as Patty began to usher Jed away and motioned for the woman to dismount. "Go over to the stables to get some fresh ones to take you home when you're done eating."

As Crissy happily complied and began leading the newcomers away, Patty turned back to Tom and Bishop. "Tom, do you think we should still—"

Tom raised a hand to effectively cut her off. "If Dillinger is getting ready to move on us, then it's all the more reason for us to speak to the town about it. Now, before it happens, Patty. Since we don't have phones or email, this is the best way to get it done."

"He's right," Bishop added.

Patty was taken aback by the tone of Bishop's voice. There had been a change in him since his son arrived. The normally somewhat passive man was on edge and it made her even more anxious. "We don't want to cause a panic," she pushed, concerned with how the fear might undermine the town.

"The only way we can possibly keep this place from being turned into a FEMA shelter is to get enough people to stand up to them," Bishop retorted with some heat. "Trying to keep the residents ignorant of what's going on won't help. It certainly won't prevent it from happening here. Dillinger might be willing to kill a couple of farmers here and there who dare to push back, but taking on a whole town is something different. I can't imagine anyone would give that order, or that enough of his men would follow it."

Patty wrung her hands together as she looked at Tom, evaluating his reaction. She knew the man well enough to recognize the resolve on his face. Nodding slowly, she did her best to stay focused on the positive. "Okay, then. There's still a lot of work to do over the next few hours before everyone starts arriving. Let's make sure we show them how strong we can be together."

Turning from the men and horses, Patty concentrated on her breathing. She knew the lack of sleep only added to her state of anxiety. Three hours in the basement while listening to Caleb tap away on his radio wasn't enough. She only had herself to blame for feeling overwhelmed. Straightening her back, Patty forced herself to walk with more purpose. The role of goodwill ambassador was a self-imposed penance, and one that she would carry out whether she felt like it or not.

Patty headed for the broad front stairs of City Hall. There was something she needed to do.

"Patty!" a grating voice called before she'd reached the second step.

Closing her eyes, Patty set her lips in a thin line. She turned to face Gary's wife, prepared to defend herself and the new mayor. In spite of riders being sent out to all of the council members' houses the night before with a notice for the unplanned meeting that morning, Gary hadn't shown up. Patty assumed it was an intentional stance to silently show his opposition, and now Emma was there to do the real talking for him.

"Have you seen Gary?" Emma asked. She glanced around nervously at all of the activity in the town square. "When he didn't come home last night, I assumed he was staying in town again, because of all of—this," she added, flinging her hands around. "Except, now I can't find him."

Patty frowned, unsure of how to answer. "Emma, Gary wasn't

very happy with the council after the last meeting yesterday morning, so I haven't spoken to him since then. Why don't you try over at The Last Stop?" When Emma scowled at the suggestion that her husband might have spent the night at a bar, Patty sighed. "I only meant that maybe he stopped in for a drink and someone might have seen him or talked to him."

Emma glared at Patty and stuck her hands on her hips. "If Gary is in that place, it's only because you drove him there."

Any other day, Patty might have laughed as she watched Emma stomp off. Instead, the encounter created another layer of disquiet that followed her up the stairs. Once inside the darkened halls of the antiquated building, Patty was more relaxed, and by the time she reached her old office she was smiling again.

Approaching the whiteboard, she was relieved to see that Sam had left her numbers in the top right corner when he'd cleaned his writing off it. Grabbing a marker, Patty's smile broadened. Finally, with their first successful delivery since the flashpoint, she was able to add to it instead of taking away. She didn't know if the 1st Force Recon Unit or Senator Jenson were going to stay, but for the time being, she also considered them a part of Mercy.

Using her fingers to rub away the numbers 638, Patty replaced them with 647. They were growing. Mercy was growing, and she would do whatever was necessary to make sure it continued.

CHAPTER 20

ETHAN
Natural Spring, Mercy, Montana

"WE CAN STAY," Ethan offered. They had just finished getting the second load of water secured and Tane was ready to head out. The only other person helping that morning besides him and Chloe was a woman who worked daily at the spring. "Why don't you ride into town and help unload?" he said to her with a smile, hoping she'd understand he was trying to prevent Tane from doing too much physical labor. "Then you can make it in time before the barbeque starts."

"I'd like that," the woman answered pleasantly with a coy wink to Ethan. "My kids are going to be waiting for me."

"You sure?" Tane asked from his perch on the wagon as the woman climbed up beside him. "If you want to ride back in too, I don't mind coming out one more time. I'm sure Danny will save me some food and I can manage the refilling on my own."

Tane referred to the impressive system Bishop helped design.

There were two raised platforms that held containers fastened to a base which slid in and out of the wagon once it was lined up, so you could back right into it. Thanks to a leverage system, it only took two people to operate it, along with the driver. While one of the plastic tubs was being used to deliver water, the other could be refilled. The only downfall was that, in spite of endless troubleshooting, the simple plumbing would constantly lose its siphon due to fluctuations in the spring's pressure, so the water flow needed to be monitored. They had to refill the empty container Tane had just swapped out so it would be ready for a quick delivery later that night, after the party.

"Go ahead!" Chloe shouted, already waving goodbye. "This won't take long and we'll meet you there. Save us a couple of seats at the table."

As the wagon lumbered away, Ethan watched Chloe skip across the open field to where their horses were tethered, calling to Grace as she went. The retriever had been acting weird all morning, hovering around the horses and sniffing at the ground. Ethan guessed it was due to the incoming storm, but the dog's restlessness was starting to rub off on him.

Giving Tango an absent pat on the head, Chloe opened her saddle bags and removed what looked like two red scarves. Narrowing his eyes, Ethan couldn't imagine what she was up to. But that was part of the reason why he liked her. "Hey," he called out as she returned. "I don't remember giving you that shirt."

Chloe looked down innocently at the brown T-shirt with the words "I aim to misbehave" on it. "Oh, really? Pretty sure you did."

Ethan emphatically shook his head. "It's my best *Firefly* shirt," he said, referencing their mutually favorite T.V. show.

"I know," Chloe said unapologetically. "Here."

Still frowning though not really mad, Ethan took the roughly cut scarf. Chloe must have made it from a scrap of one of his grandma's sewing projects, causing his curiosity to deepen. Turning it over in his hands, he couldn't help but smile when he saw the logo on it. It was made from a crude piece of colored, cut-out cardboard that was glued on, and it was the coolest thing ever. The green triangle with yellow stripes and blue star was the emblem for the rebel soldiers from the same show, called Browncoats. Red scarves were also originally part of their basic uniforms. Ethan immediately got the reference and how it might apply to their current situation in Mercy, what with being rising rebels and all. "So, why Browncoats and not the Rebel Alliance?" he teased, not willing to let her off so easily.

Chloe rolled her eyes as she dramatically draped the scarf around her neck. "I considered it, but decided the brown robes would be too restrictive if we ever really got into a fight."

Ethan put his own scarf on and nodded thoughtfully. "True, but not all Jedi's wear robes."

They continued their debate as they went back to where the container was sitting and began the process of filling it. Ethan was glad she was in such a good mood. After the night before, he didn't know what to expect.

Once his dad was done with his "trust" lecture and Ethan convinced him he was jumping to the wrong conclusions about his alone time with Chloe, he'd gone back to the barn to help finish up with the hay. Chloe and Bishop were in the middle of a pretty heated conversation, so he'd made himself scarce. He knew they had things to work out and since he wasn't really a part of it, thought it would be best not to bring it up unless Chloe offered first.

Ethan wasn't sure if it was a normal response, but he didn't really care one way or another about Bishop, James, and the whole political mess with the senator. The only thing that interested him was the seed vault. Since Bishop was basically the reason they knew about it, he was glad the guy was some secret-agent dude. It meant Sam would have his indoor gardens, and the rest of them would be eating next year. Oh…and Dillinger. He also hoped having the recon guys there meant they could trounce the jerk whenever he showed up.

"Earth to Ethan," Chloe sang while moving her hand back and forth in front of his face. "We need to pump it again, space cadet."

Offering her a crooked grin, Ethan jumped down from where they stood on the platform. A very basic handpump was rigged up, connected to flexible plastic tubing that trailed from the bottom of the filtration system. Grabbing the pump, he got the water flowing again and then studied the level in the large plastic tub. "It's already close to half-filled," he said, scrambling back up next to Chloe. Licking his lips, he made a dramatic smacking sound. "I'm ready for another round of steaks."

Chloe smiled and then raised her eyebrows playfully at him. "How about a side trip first?" She gestured over her shoulder toward the entrance to the mine. "You still owe me a tour."

Ethan hesitated, and glanced up at the clouds that had continued to grow in intensity over the past two days. "Maybe," he muttered, not sure why he suddenly felt so uneasy. It was as if the atmosphere shifted like before with the last storm, causing a heaviness in the air and a prickling along his spine. He looked to make sure his rifle was in its scabbard on Tango and noticed Grace was still pacing, adding to his foreboding. Turning back, he found Chloe watching him expectantly and he tried to shrug it off. "I hope it doesn't rain on the party."

CHAPTER 21

DANNY
City Center, Mercy, Montana

"WHAT I'M ASKING from each of you is a commitment to work together!"

The crowd around Danny cheered again. The response to Tom's speech was incredibly positive and he had to yell to be heard beyond the courtyard and out onto Main Street, where the population of Mercy overflowed.

Danny was amazed by the turnout. She thought Patty had been going overboard when she saw all the tables lining the sidewalks of Main Street, but now she wasn't sure if it was going to be enough. To see so many people thriving in spite of what had happened was truly inspiring.

"If you haven't already been assigned something to work on, please see the people stationed along the side of the town square. There are signs posted identifying the various programs and projects." Tom gestured to the tables and then raised both of his hands over his head. "Most importantly, because of the actions of the military I've already described to you, we need anyone willing to act as part of a town guard. Especially those of you with any military, police, or security experience."

A murmur rose through the throng of people gathered and Danny could feel an element of fear thread its way into the excitement. She understood the apprehension, and figured it might not be a bad thing. Fear had a way of compelling people to act.

Danny spotted her dad moving through the crowd, his head several inches taller than most of the people around him. Waving a hand, she jumped up and down to get his attention, wincing at the pain it provoked. "Over here, Dad!" she shouted during a lull. She saw him pull up at the water station earlier, right before the speech started, and was glad he didn't miss all of it.

Tom raised his hands again and the hum subsided as everyone strained to listen. "Mercy *will* be free!" Tom smiled as several people shouted in agreement. "Just as our forefathers guaranteed our independence from tyranny nearly two hundred and fifty years ago, we will remain united and free!"

Danny wasn't sure if Tom had intended for that to be the end of his speech, but as people cheered and applauded, it was impossible for him to say anything further. She was glad Ethan had talked her into letting Grace go with him and Chloe to the spring; the retriever would have been overwhelmed by all of the people and noise. Thinking of the two, she looked around, wondering where they were.

"The kids back?" she hollered to her dad while leaning in close to him.

Tane nodded, putting an arm around her shoulders so they could talk. "They should be here soon. Let's go find our seats while Tom finishes his rally."

Danny grinned at her dad, glad to see him making jokes. She didn't know how he could be so calm in light of everything that was going on, including being on the last dose of his heart medicine. Melissa was working on coming up with some natural supplements to help offset the symptoms that were bound to show up with a vengeance, though it did little to calm her nerves. It was imperative they come up with a way to find it, in addition to all the other meds that were needed.

Two guitar players took Tom's place on stage and they began a rendition of a popular, patriotic country song. Danny moved to meet him at the foot of the platform, but Sheriff Waters ran up and cut her off, radio in hand.

"We have a sighting," he announced, not bothering to try and keep it a secret. "A lookout positioned just beyond the south gate. Estimates a good two dozen armed soldiers on horseback."

One of the guitar players must have overhead because he faltered in his strumming and stared down at them in alarm. "The soldiers are here already?" he shouted.

Tom sighed and rushed back out onto the stage. "Everyone, stay calm! Please, remain here and we'll do our best to take care of this."

Danny fell in behind Tom and his entourage as they pushed their way through the swarm of people. Once on Main Street, movement became easier, and a deputy waited for them with their horses a few blocks away.

Danny rested a hand on Lilly's neck as she watched James and his men get organized. Apparently, they didn't go anywhere without their gear close by because they were already looking like G.I. Joe action figures. When the soldiers opted to stay on foot and began walking down the road, Tom led Lilly by the reins so he and Danny could continue talking.

Once they neared the roadblock, he became increasingly

antsy. "I'm not even going to try and tell you guys what to do," Tom said to Danny as he glanced over her shoulder.

Turning, Danny saw that Sandy and Senator Jenson were catching up to them and she grinned back at Tom. "Good idea. I don't think any of us would listen."

"Will you at least stay back and let Bishop and James try to do the talking first?" he said, including his mom in the conversation as she pulled Senator Jenson along by the arm. He gestured to the politician. "We don't want to show all of our cards up front."

"I'm more than happy to let the guys flex their muscles at each other for a while," the senator replied, and Danny raised her eyebrows at the woman.

"Senator, I've met Dillinger," Danny cautioned. "This isn't a guy who's all show and no bite."

"Unfortunately, Danny is right," James added, slapping a magazine into place on his assault rifle. "A show of force up front is the best way to approach him."

Danny looked at the six soldiers and knew they would be outnumbered at least three to one. Hicks also had an AR, but Tom, Bishop, the Sheriff, and his two deputies only had pistols or rifles.

"Chief Martinez and Sam are working on rounding up some help," Sheriff Waters said while climbing onto his horse. "But if what you're saying is true, James, it would be best if we're all waiting for them at the gate when they get there."

"Give me your radio," Danny said to Waters while holding out her hand. When the sheriff glanced at Tom before complying, she was unable to hide her annoyance. "You don't need two radios with you! We'll hang back out of sight, and if the corporal decides he wants to have a conversation with our senator here, you can let us know."

Tom, clearly relieved to have his mom and Danny not

pushing to be a part of the confrontation, took Waters radio when he offered it, and handed it to her. As her hand wrapped around it, instead of letting go, he pulled her towards him. Kissing her briefly, he then pressed his forehead against hers, sharing the same breath with her for a moment.

"Be careful," she whispered. "And I've got your back," she added, shaking the radio at him as he pulled away.

Sandy set a hand on her shoulder as the men continued down the road, both on foot and horseback. She appreciated the small gesture of support. Sandy was the type of woman Danny imagined her own mother would be, if not for the addiction that took over her life. Reaching up to grasp Sandy's hand, she was going to say thank you but was stopped by a panicked voice on the radio.

"North gate to...anyone. We have a large group of soldiers approaching. We—"

"North gate, repeat your traffic!" Tom's voice squawked.

Danny watched as the group stopped in the road, some distance from their goal. Tom was twisted around in his saddle and looking back in their direction. Had they been tricked somehow, and Dillinger was at the north end of town, instead of the south?

Then, the unmistakable sound of horses approaching began to rumble from nearby, growing louder by the second. Confused, Danny took several steps in Tom's direction, and squinted at the guards standing near the gate a couple hundred feet away. First, there was a plume of dust and then the first row of horses came into view, all ridden by soldiers in combat gear.

"I've got a sergeant here who says he's from the Malmstrom base."

Danny stared at the radio in horror as the realization of what was happening became apparent.

The radio clicked again and the guard's broken voice gave

confirmation. *"Says he's here by order of a General Montgomery and we're to surrender the town."*

Danny looked first at Sandy and then Senator Jenson, holding the radio out like it had turned into a snake in her hands. "We're surrounded."

CHAPTER 22

Tom

South Gate, Mercy, Montana

Tom's initial reaction was humiliation at being so easily overrun. He wanted to be angry with Bishop and James for not anticipating the move and countering it before it had happened. However, as he watched Dillinger riding toward them, he accepted the fact that they were in an impossible situation.

James and his men had arrived less than twenty-four hours ago. They'd already increased the lookouts and guards in the town and were actively recruiting their own army. There was nothing else they could have done in such a short amount of time.

"Dillinger." James spat the name like it was something vile and took a step forward so that he was in front of everyone.

Tom dismounted and withdrew his rifle from its scabbard before he and Bishop took a position to either side of James. Tom waited in apprehension as the corporal continued his approach. Raising the radio, he said the only thing he could think of to the guard at the north gate. "Tell the sergeant to standby. We're meeting with Corporal Dillinger now."

Bishop nodded at Tom in approval. "Tell him we'll advise them of the corporal's orders. That'll buy us some more time."

"More time for what?" Tom asked, but keyed the radio up before getting an answer. "I'll advise you of the corporal's orders." He shrugged at Bishop as he clipped the radio back onto his jeans. It didn't matter what the response was.

He glanced over his shoulder to reassure himself that Danny and his mom were out of direct view. Danny must have been watching him closely, because she raised a hand when he turned, confirming they were in the shadows on the porch of a small, abandoned real estate office. He felt some relief knowing that Ethan and Chloe were at least far removed from it at the spring.

They had left the buildings of Main Street behind and now were primarily surrounded by wilderness and very few structures. However, Tom was painfully aware of how close the water station and City Hall were. It wouldn't take long for Dillinger's troops to reach all of it if they were overpowered.

"Tom, do you copy? Tom!" Sam's voice was barely audible as he yelled into the radio.

Tom snagged the radio without looking away from the road and the soldiers coming closer to the gate separating them. "What is it, Sam?"

"We've got some reinforcements for you. We're on our way."

Uncertain exactly what Sam meant by reinforcements, Tom tried to think clearly about the best way to use the extra help. "Split anyone you've got between us and the north gate. Out." He could hear more chatter but ignored it. It was too late to do anything else.

"Whoa," Dillinger called out as he pulled his horse to stop and held a hand up to direct his men to do the same. "What have we here?"

It was obvious to Tom that the corporal was surprised to be met with any kind of organized resistance, but he still had a smirk on his face. It was as if he found the whole thing amusing. Tom felt his cheeks burning and it was all he could do not to shove his way past James and pull the arrogant man off his horse.

"Master Sergeant James Campbell, 1st Force Reconnaissance," James barked, sounding steady and dangerous. "State your business here, Corporal."

Dillinger shifted in his saddle and studied the sergeant like he was an oddity. Even from a distance of more than twenty feet, Tom could see the mockery on the corporal's face. "I didn't think we'd be meeting again so soon, Sergeant. How about we drop the formalities and be frank with each other? You decided to take a little field trip." Dillinger wrinkled his nose at the trees and visible landscape. "Can't say it would have been my first choice."

"The sergeant gave you an order!" Bishop snapped.

Tom was startled by the iron authority Bishop emanated and he stole a glance at the older man. He was standing rigid in what Tom assumed was "at attention" in military jargon, and his gaze was fixed on Dillinger. He left no doubt, even without a uniform, that he outranked everyone there.

Dillinger sat a little straighter and took a moment to put it together. Tom had to give him credit for taking it all in stride. "You must be the elusive Colonel Campbell." He smiled broadly. "I can see the family resemblance now. Well, that's going to make things so much easier. Good job finding your father, Sergeant. I assume the senator is somewhere nearby, too?"

"Let's cut through the bullshit so everyone here is clear about some things," Tom shouted. He was pretty sure he heard both

James and Bishop grunt in disapproval as he marched past them, but this was his town and Tom wasn't going to play games. He certainly wasn't going to play Dillinger's game.

"My name is Thomas Miller and I'm the mayor of Mercy. This man behind me is Sheriff Waters." Ignoring Dillinger, Tom focused on each of the men fanned out behind him on horseback. He recognized a few of them from FEMA Shelter M3. That was good. "This is a community with a population of more than six hundred people and it's my responsibility to speak on their behalf. I'm informing you that we do not need, nor do we require your assistance. Based on your violent takeovers of other towns and farms, you're not welcome here."

Dillinger scoffed, but several of his soldiers turned to look at each other with uncertainty. Tom figured it was one thing to overreact in the heat of a fight and kill a random farmer or two, but to summarily gun down a mayor and sheriff protecting their town? These were men and women who also had families and Tom was praying they still had some integrity left.

Dillinger slowly nodded, tsking at Tom as he slid a leg over and dropped down from his horse. "I gotta hand it to you, Miller. You got some steel ones. Unfortunately, all it's going to accomplish is getting you killed." Any remnant of humor left the corporal's face as he took a marked step toward Tom. "You want me to be blunt? Okay, here's how this is going to go: you and your posse are going to lay down your weapons and allow these troops to carry out our orders. If you don't comply, you will be shot. Your farm will be destroyed, and I will see to it personally that your family is killed in the middle of Main Street as an example to the rest of your precious town. Is that clear enough for you?"

Tom clenched his teeth against the surge of rage and adrenaline, his nostrils flaring. He heard James raise his rifle just before the rush of blood in his ears muted everything else out. Grunting in frustration, Tom lost his inner battle and lunged forward as Bishop and Waters both grabbed at his arms. Realizing he was playing right into Dillinger's plan, Tom allowed his friends to drag him back as the corporal began to laugh.

"You don't want to do this," James said loudly, ignoring Tom's outburst and addressing the group of soldiers. "Your orders aren't as clear as you all believe them to be. You might outnumber us, but I'll guarantee my men will be cleaning you off their boots at the end of the day if this goes sideways."

Dillinger's smile faltered under the validity of James's statement, and he eyed the rifle that was pointed in his direction. Before he could come up with a response, the unexpected sound of a distant helicopter began to echo through the valley.

"I'm good," Tom muttered, shrugging off Bishop and the sheriff. "But we need to end this."

As some of the soldiers became distracted and began to look around for the source, Tom heard another unusual sound coming down the street from the direction of Mercy. Not wanting to turn away from the ongoing stand-off, he was startled when Danny called out from close by.

"We've got some more people that have something to say about all of this," she announced.

Dillinger was the first to react, his smile turning to a scowl. He began yelling as an orange flash of lightning from the looming thunderstorm punctuated his words. "This doesn't change your orders! Do not stand down. Mercy *will* surrender to us!"

Confused, Tom turned enough to look behind him and was startled to see Danny and Sam leading a group of at least fifty men and women. They all held a variety of weapons ranging from pistols and rifles, to shovels and picks. Adding to the baffling scene was the party attire some of them wore. Their red-white-and-blue shirts and hats made the assembly look like they were marching in a parade, rather than into battle.

Sam pointed his shovel at Dillinger and then waved it over his head. "You're going to have to go through all of us first!"

*J*AMES
    Master Sergeant, US Marines, 1ˢᵗ Force Reconnaissance
South gate, Mercy, Montana

JAMES DIDN'T LIKE the odds, but his team was used to being outnumbered and with their backs against the wall. If it weren't for the civilians in harm's way, he would've already opened fire. He appreciated what the townspeople were doing, though the reality was that they were likely only making the situation more convoluted and with the same outcome in the end. Dillinger wasn't there to negotiate. He was out for blood, and James was more than willing to give him what he wanted.

Dillinger was on the verge of reaching for his own weapon when the Huey came into view. The corporal's demeanor instantly changed, and it was obvious he knew who was making the insane landing on the narrow road. Furious, Dillinger grabbed at his horse to keep it from running away as dirt and debris flew around them.

James exchanged a knowing look with his father as they all lowered their weapons to the ready position. There weren't many running helicopters, and one of them was sitting abandoned over thirty miles to the north of them. He could only think of one man who would have the reach to pull off such a stunt.

"Montgomery," Bishop snarled as The Man in the Mountain himself emerged from the bird, trailing several more armed soldiers behind him.

While most of the troops were still on horseback, they nonetheless attempted to come to attention and salute the general as he made his way toward Dillinger. The corporal, on the other hand, was clearly annoyed and wasn't trying to hide it.

"General!" Corporal Dillinger barked, finally throwing him a disingenuous salute. "I wasn't expecting you to oversee this operation in person. I was going to notify you later today of our successful reconnaissance in Mercy."

The general raised an eyebrow at Dillinger, and James saw a glimmer of hope. Recon? The corporal might be even further outside his scope of command than they'd suspected if he was only supposed to observe and report.

"The same success you had at the Duke Ranch?" Montgomery shot back. The Huey was winding down, making it possible to talk without shouting, though the general's voice was more than loud enough for everyone to hear. "Or how about the Pony Express station? Because we just came from there, and I have to say your idea of a successful command is perhaps different than mine."

Dillinger's face burned red and he had the common sense to accept the general's words without any argument. Instead, he gestured to Tom and James and the people standing behind them. "Sir, as you can see the quarantine clearly isn't valid. We're ready to take control of the town and establish FEMA Shelter M4 and Command Three."

Montgomery stepped around the barrier and stopped mere feet from James, tugging once at his jacket before focusing his steely gaze on him. "Master Sergeant Campbell, this is going to go one of two ways for you. I'll even give you a few minutes to think about it. Colonel Campbell," he continued, pivoting toward Bishop.

As Montgomery spoke his father's name, Colonel Walsh's head jerked up and he stared wide-eyed at Bishop. James squinted at the man, trying to measure his reaction. He had to know about the seed vault, and therefore the value of finding his dad alive. As far as Montgomery and his henchmen knew, his dad could be the only person left on the planet capable of opening the vaults and that made him very, very valuable.

"General," Bishop answered with a brisk nod of his head. "I think we have some things to talk about, and I'd rather not do it this way."

"Make no mistake," Montgomery said smoothly, glancing at each of the men in front of him, including Tom. "I might not agree with some of the colonel's tactics, but he's a means to an end that must and will come to pass. I see the rumors of your outbreak have been greatly exaggerated, Mr. Miller."

James willed Tom to keep his cool as he did his best to evaluate the six new soldiers that arrived with Montgomery. Just as he feared, they weren't random grunts like Dillinger's troops, and were likely special ops. In view of the gear they sported, he suspected they were SEALs. Not good.

"We're managing," Tom answered evenly. "I was just informing your messenger boy that we're doing fine on our own.

If you'd like to discuss a possible collaboration with Mercy, I'd be happy to set up a meeting to go over some options."

General Montgomery chuckled. "I think you might be confused, though Corporal Dillinger advised me that you're a rather intelligent man. Maybe you just aren't well-versed on how martial law works. Unfortunately, I don't have the time or patience to explain it to you. However, I will give you the option of having your men move this barricade aside so we can still do this peacefully. None of us want any bloodshed," he continued, focusing on Bishop.

James sensed they were at a pivotal moment. He briefly considered putting a bullet in both Montgomery and Dillinger's heads. He'd likely get the shots off before someone was able to take him out. His hand twitched on the butt of his weapon as he clenched his teeth together and fought against the desire to carry it out.

While eliminating them might stop the immediate threat against Mercy, James had no idea who else was involved in the general's plans. It would only serve to fuel the argument being made for the existence of the FEMA shelters and continued martial law. The resulting gunfire would likely get most of them killed, destroying the ability for anyone to access the seed vaults, and silencing the strongest proponent for the civilian government.

James's internal debate helped make some things clear to him. It was only a split-second of introspection, but it was enough. There were bigger things at play worthy of a worldwide stage, and his goal shifted to the prevention of anyone dying that day.

The general must have noticed the slight shift in his body language, or perhaps the way James lowered his rifle a couple more inches. He was a master at reading people and it was partly how he'd come to be a four-star general. "Sergeant," he said, his voice sharp and demanding. "I trust the senator is well?"

"I'm actually quite exceptional," Senator Jenson called out from somewhere in the crowd of people who filled the street behind them. James managed to keep his expression neutral and resisted the urge to turn around. He saw Tom stiffen when Danny and the senator walked up to join them, but he agreed with the ploy. Moving against a US senator added another layer to an already messy scenario. Based on Walsh's reaction, it was exactly what they needed. The man was looking increasingly apprehensive.

"I heard you were looking for me," Senator Jenson said pleasantly. "The sergeant here and his men were kind enough to make sure I stayed safe."

The first trace of irritation flickered across General Montgomery's face as the woman's obstinance rattled his resolve. James knew the general was being forced into an unexpected crossroads. He'd have to choose between maintaining his façade of civility and try to manipulate his way into controlling the seed vault, or else take it all by force and declare open war against the civilian government. Either way, as far as Montgomery was concerned, everyone there was expendable except for Bishop. He knew he'd have to take him alive in order to control the vaults and the seat of power he'd been carefully creating.

James couldn't let him do that.

In one fluid movement, he reached out and swept his father behind him while yelling to his men. "On me!"

Nothing else needed to be said as all five Alpha units and Hicks formed a protective barrier around Bishop. His dad was smart enough to understand what James was doing and didn't try to resist. So long as they had Bishop, they still maintained some control. Slowly, James began to back away.

"Think carefully right now, Sergeant," General Montgomery shouted, motioning for the six SEALs to advance. "You took an oath. If you hand over the senator and your father, we can avoid an unnecessary and rather pointless conflict. Otherwise, I will have you and your men arrested for treason."

A hand rested on James's shoulder and he was reassured that Jay was there and had his back. "We're with you, Sarge."

"Always have been," Lucas added.

James stopped and raised a closed fist, a sudden gust of wind swirling dry leaves and pine needles around them. Meeting Tom's gaze he recognized the same feral instinct he felt, to do whatever was necessary to protect the people he loved. James wasn't just fighting for his father, but also his wife and little girl, who he'd left alone and vulnerable hundreds of miles away. If he allowed Montgomery to succeed, he might as well be putting them into a camp, too, without any guarantee of food or protection. It had to stop there, in Mercy. It was time to make a stand.

"I'm the bargaining chip," his dad whispered from close behind him. "You're the ace up our sleeve they don't know about. Let's use that. I'll go with them for now to buy us some time. You're the one who has to live, James. You can control the vault."

He didn't want to listen to his dad, but as a soldier, James knew he was right. Bishop pushed his way around him to stand next to Tom, directly across from Montgomery. Standing tall, he raised his chin and spoke with a clarity that left no doubt as to whether he was bluffing. "The only way you'll ever find and get into the vault is by working with me, General. Pull back your troops and I'll go with you. If you truly serve the people, then you'll stop this madness and work with us."

James was vaguely aware of more horses coming around the helicopter as he leveled his rifle at Montgomery. He heard his men mirror his actions, which caused the SEALs to raise their weapons in response. One by one, the rest of the people in the road followed suit; some of them out of fear, duty, or the simple desire to be free.

James was okay with dying that day, especially since he was

surrounded by people he respected, including his father. But he was counting on the fact that the general couldn't risk losing Bishop and that the man hadn't completely lost his mind, after all. Taking a steady breath, he delivered what might be his last words. "Order your men to stand down...*sir.*"

CHAPTER 24

CHLOE

Natural Spring, Mercy, Montana

THE WATER WAS FINALLY TOPPED off, after stopping for what Chloe would have sworn was more than a dozen times. "You'd think," she said to Ethan with heavy sarcasm, "that as smart as Bishop and Sam are, they'd be able to fix something so simple."

Ethan pointed at the water that was constantly flowing from the natural spring and down through the man-made filtering contraption. "Sam said it would require a pressure system to regulate the flow enough."

"Yeah, I know," Chloe quipped, waving a hand. "It's all basic physics involving PSI and flow rate and the fact we have no electricity or working electronics."

Ethan stopped following her back to the horses and crossed his arms over his chest, frowning. "If you already know all of that, then why complain?"

Chloe turned back to face him with a look of amusement. "It

wasn't so much a complaint as an observation. And the fact that I'm sick of literally watching water move. Come on!" she added with some urgency, reaching out to punch his arm before running away. "Cave time!"

When Ethan didn't follow right away, she skidded to a stop and squinted at him. He was grimacing and rubbing his arm, and Chloe could tell he was trying to think of something witty to say in order to change her mind. "Why don't you want to go?"

Ethan shrugged. "It's just a cave."

Her eyes narrowing further, Chloe jutted her chin out. "You've been going on and on about how cool Henry's Hollow is for the past three days. I wanna see the old stuff in there before it gets cleaned out and turned into a field."

Glancing first at the clouds that were continuing to build, and then at Grace, who had moved her focus beyond the horses and was sniffing around the entrance to the mine, Ethan finally reached out and took her hand. "My dad will kill me if he finds out."

"So, he doesn't find out." Chloe didn't understand his sudden lack of adventure.

"Somehow, he always knows when I do things." Ethan pulled his hand back and jammed both of them into his back pockets, making him look much closer to his real age. "Trying to lie to him is pointless."

Chloe laughed. "I didn't realize you were so…*good.*"

"I'm not," Ethan scoffed. "I just have a very strong sense of self-preservation."

"Fine." Chloe looped an arm through Ethan's and tugged to get him walking again. "We won't go all the way in. Just to the entrance of it, okay? It's only a couple hundred feet inside the mine, isn't it? That way, if your dad asks, we can honestly say we didn't go into the cave."

While Ethan didn't look completely swayed by her argument,

he allowed Chloe to pull him along and was smiling again by the time they reached Grace. He had mentioned how weird she was acting, and Chloe had to agree. The retriever sat with her haunches shaking when they approached her, making an unusual whining sound.

"I don't think she should go with us," Ethan said, petting her on the head. "What if she tries to fetch a stick of dynamite or something?"

Chloe was thinking the same thing. "Yeah, let's have her stay with the horses."

A gust of wind swirled through the glade, carrying with it the unmistakable smell of coming rain. Chloe wouldn't have ever believed it was possible to say she could smell the rain, but after being in the mountains for a month, she understood the saying and knew it was totally true. Grace jumped up and sniffed furiously at the wind before whining again, convincing Chloe that they were in for one doozy of a storm. "We'll make it quick," she said to Ethan. "Promise."

Ethan had to take Grace back and tell her to stay three times before she listened, and Chloe was about to give up on the cave exploration idea when he finally succeeded. She wasn't sure why seeing Henry's Hollow was so important to her. It was just that she'd been thinking about it for several days, and was afraid once the work started, they'd never get a chance to be there alone again. Hearing Ethan describe it to her had built it up in her mind so that it was like fulfilling a dare, more than anything. There was something about traipsing inside a mine they'd been told to stay out of that was so...*normal* that Chloe couldn't pass it up.

The early afternoon light was already fading, thanks to the clouds, when Ethan led the way inside the mine opening. The two-by-fours that were previously secured in place had already been removed, so there wasn't anything barring their way. Chloe instantly wished she'd thought ahead and brought a light with them, though they could still see well enough to enable them to follow the tunnel wall.

"Ever been in a cave?" Ethan asked, glancing back at her. She must have looked scared, because he took her hand and gave her a crooked grin. "You're the one who wanted to do this."

Doing her best to ignore the roughly contoured rock ceiling that was way too close to her head, Chloe tossed the loose flap of her scarf over her shoulder and kept moving. "Having a natural fear of small spaces doesn't mean I don't want to see this magical cave."

Ethan winced and wiped at his nose. "Um, yeah. About that. I might have built it up slightly more than is justified."

Raising her eyebrows, Chloe dropped his hand and pushed at Ethan's back to propel him further into the tunnel. "Now I really have to see it. How much farther?"

"See that light up there?" he asked, pointing down a side tunnel they'd just come even with. "That's it."

Chloe found herself wavering at stepping into the smaller natural tunnel that led to Henry's Hollow. While it was wider than the one they were standing in, it was markedly lower, so that even she would have to duck to get through it. "Name me one movie where doing anything in a cave ends well," she muttered.

Ethan was already several steps in and twisted around to smile back at her, his face hard to see in the dim light so that it was mostly his teeth that stood out. "You're being dramatic."

"Am I?" she pushed, stepping in after him. "Name one, then." As he began their trek forward again, Chloe found that the farther they got, the more she agreed with his original assessment that it might not be a good idea. However, her stubborn streak prevented her from conceding and admitting he was right.

Ethan snapped his fingers, making her jump. "I got it! Pretty much all of the SG1 episodes."

"You're seriously going to try and bring *Stargate* into this?" Chloe was still fighting against a wave of claustrophobia, but the conversation was distracting her enough so that it wasn't consuming her. "First of all, they were in a man-made bunker inside a mountain."

"Cheyenne Mountain," Ethan added.

Chloe rolled her eyes, even though he couldn't see it. "Duh. Were you not listening to James last night? Even without his true horror stories, literally every *Stargate* episode involved some worldwide threat."

Ethan stopped at the threshold to the cave, staring at her. She smiled mockingly at him, proud she had finally stumped him with something. Stepping up next to him, she was startled by how bright it was in the huge cavern, due to several large beams of natural light cutting wide swaths through the darkness.

Chloe stepped a few feet inside the cave before taking it all in, moving into the nearest shaft of light and welcoming the false sense of warmth and security it offered. As she looked up and closed her eyes, there was a distinct clicking sound from some-where close by that echoed through the hollow. Gasping at the realization they weren't alone; Chloe opened her eyes at the same time that Ethan grabbed and pulled her protectively against him.

They spun together to face where the sound had come from, and Chloe was utterly confused when she saw Father Russell standing in the shadows. Old tools were scattered in the dirt at his feet, and stacks of wooden crates loomed behind him. Clus-ters of odd wires fanned out around the priest, trailing across the ground to disappear into the darkness. It took a moment for Chloe to realize he was holding a gun and although it didn't make any sense, it was most definitely pointed at them.

"Well, now. This is unfortunate." His voice was so pleasant that it only added to the bizarre scene, making Chloe feel like they'd fallen down the rabbit hole.

Swallowing hard, she reached for Ethan's hand. "Why do I always have to be right?"

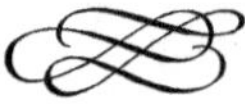

CHAPTER 25

E THAN

Henry's Hollow, Mercy, Montana

ETHAN GRIPPED Chloe's hand and tried to pull her back through the opening, but Russell anticipated the move and thrust the gun at them threateningly.

Moving with an uncanny grace, he narrowed the distance between them. "Uh-uh," Russell uttered, shaking his head. "Don't. You're both going to die here today, though I'd rather not shoot you." He gestured with his free hand to the wooden boxes behind him. "Ricocheting bullets could have a rather spectacular outcome."

"What are you doing?" Chloe sputtered, her normally cool exterior gone.

"Isn't it obvious?" When neither Ethan or Chloe answered him, Russell sighed audibly and shook his head. "I'm rather disappointed, Ethan. I suspected you were one of the...worthy. I recognized something in you," he continued, using the gun for emphasis as he jabbed it at Ethan. "You and I, we aren't so different."

A deep-seated fear began to slowly slither up from Ethan's gut to settle in his chest, making it difficult to breathe. The shadowy chamber, with the shafts of light fading and brightening as the clouds swiftly passed overhead outside, could have been the location of any number of Ethan's recent nightmares. In them, instead of Decker or Billy doing the killing, it was him. When he woke drenched in sweat in the middle of the night, it was because of his revulsion at the pleasure he felt committing the heinous acts. Ethan's terror was that he wasn't any better than the killers who had kidnapped him and he'd never be able to outrun the truth. For a heartbeat, it felt like the priest was looking into his soul and calling him out. Only, that wasn't possible and Ethan knew he was projecting his own fears into the situation to try and make sense of it. The man was crazy.

Russell grinned then, a morbid expression when combined with the weapon and maniacal energy in his eyes. "You get to be a part of something exceptional."

"You're not a priest!" Chloe spat, her anger beginning to override her horror. "And I'm not sure what kind of twisted complex you have, but you and Ethan are nothing alike."

"I'm certain a long discussion with you on abnormal psychology would be thrilling, Chloe, but I'm afraid I've got a schedule to keep." Russell continued to speak like he hadn't just threatened their lives and was holding a gun on them. "So I'm going to need you to come over here and sit down next to this cart."

When Chloe balked and took another step back, Russell reacted with lightning speed, leaping forward and striking Ethan against the temple. Pain exploded through his head and he staggered sideways, bumping into Chloe and knocking them both to the ground.

"Umph," Ethan grunted as the second impact caused another fresh burst of pain in his forehead.

Chloe scrambled out from under him and began to pull at his shoulders, trying to drag him away from Russell. "Come on!" she whimpered, looking back-and-forth between him and Russell. Her eyes were wide with a stark terror Ethan had seen before. He looked away and shook his head in an attempt to clear it. He had to focus.

"Here." Something hit his legs as Russell spoke, making Ethan flinch as he turned back to see a length of rope in his lap. "Tie him up or I put a bullet in his head."

There was something about the rope that wasn't right. It was too thin and looked more like a cord. Ethan's thoughts sharpened with the realization that it wasn't a rope. He'd seen the material before, two summers ago, when they did some blasting for an access road on the back property at the farm. His dad made a fuss about it and almost didn't let him watch. Ethan stared at the mass of cords on the ground and his breaths quickened. "Russell, what are you doing in here?"

Chloe stopped her hopeless battle to drag him and crouched down, looking like a caged animal. When Russell leveled the gun at Ethan's head, she picked up the length of cord with a strangled sob.

"I'm only doing what I must," Russell said without emotion. "Certainly, no one can deny the Earth is trying to purge itself. I'm simply playing my part."

"You aren't God!" Chloe looked up at him as she spoke and grimaced when the depth of his lunacy became apparent to them both. "How many people have you already killed?"

Shrugging, Russell kicked at Chloe's hand. "Start tying. And I have no idea at this point, though it doesn't matter. Live or die, it's the course of nature. Let's not confuse that with the will of a god created by man's inability to find their own answers."

Ethan's head hurt, but he didn't think that was the reason he was having a hard time following the man's logic. At least he was talking, which was better than killing them or blowing them up. He needed to formulate a plan, and he began eyeing the rusty tools laying nearby.

Just as Ethan spotted a potentially sharp ax-head, Chloe grasped his wrist. Propped up on one elbow, he rolled toward her, expecting her to follow the order to tie his hands together. Instead, she gave him a signal, mouthing a silent "now" before launching herself backwards into Russell while wrestling for the gun.

The distraction was all he needed. Lunging for the rusty blade, Ethan rolled to his feet. Chloe was small but wiry, and she'd gotten a good grip on the man's right arm. As Russell grabbed her by the hair with his other hand and began to haul her back, Ethan swung as hard as he could at Russell's exposed shoulder.

The blade didn't bite into the bone, but it was enough to make the gun drop from Russell's hand. It spun across the floor of the cave as he howled in pain and threw Chloe away from him. Ethan met their attacker's gaze and knew there was only one way any of them were going to make it out of the cave alive.

Lowering his shoulder, he slammed into Russell's chest, trying to tackle him to the ground.

"Umph," Russell grunted. He wrapped Ethan up and managed to stay on his feet so that Ethan only succeeded in driving him backward until they both crashed into a boulder painted with graffiti. It wasn't enough to knock the wind from the larger man, and Ethan couldn't disengage fast enough to evade a flurry of strikes to his stomach and face.

Trying to backpedal while vainly attempting to bring his arms up to block the blows, Ethan knew he was in trouble. Russell could fight, and even with an injured shoulder, Ethan was no match for him. But it didn't matter. He just had to hold out long enough for Chloe.

His lip split and Ethan's mouth filled with the taste of blood as his heartbeat pounded in his head, drowning out his ragged gasps and grunts of pain. Reversing tactics, Ethan stopped trying to get away and instead dropped low. Hugging Russell's legs, he pulled him to the ground as he shouted. "Run, Chloe. Run!"

Russell easily broke free, though there was a brief reprise as they grappled on the ground. Ethan might not be much of a fighter, but he was big, and he knew how to wrestle. Scrambling, he pushed them around in a circle on the ground, using his legs for leverage.

"Why fight it?" Russell cooed as he managed to reverse their positions and straddled Ethan. "There's no point in fighting me, boy. I was always going to come for you."

Ethan clawed at Russell's forearm as it slid around his throat, understanding that there was no tapping out of their fight.

As the edges of his vision began to gray, Ethan continued to flail and frantically tried to look around and see if Chloe had made it out of the room. She was running, only it wasn't away from them. She was coming at them, and she had the long wooden handle of the ax in her hands.

"Stop!" Chloe screamed, swinging down as she drew close.

A thudding noise, a shift of weight, and the pressure against Ethan's throat eased. His vision still blurred, he gagged several times and then tried to drag himself through the dirt. Away from Russell. He had to get away.

Another thud from nearby and then a scream. "Chloe," Ethan groaned, blinking furiously in an effort to see clearly. Hauling himself onto his hands and knees, he reached toward where he could see a flurry of movement. He heard heavy footfalls and knew Chloe was running for the tunnel. She was going to get away.

Then, he saw Russell and knew his actions were too calculated as he rose to his feet and lifted his arms in her direction.

Crack!

A muzzle flash exploded in the shadowy light of Henry's Hollow, and Ethan watched in horror as Chloe spun around from the impact of a bullet.

"No!" Ethan yelled hoarsely, unable to force his legs to hold his weight. Falling back onto his stomach in the dirt, he saw Chloe's red scarf flutter to the ground next to where she lay.

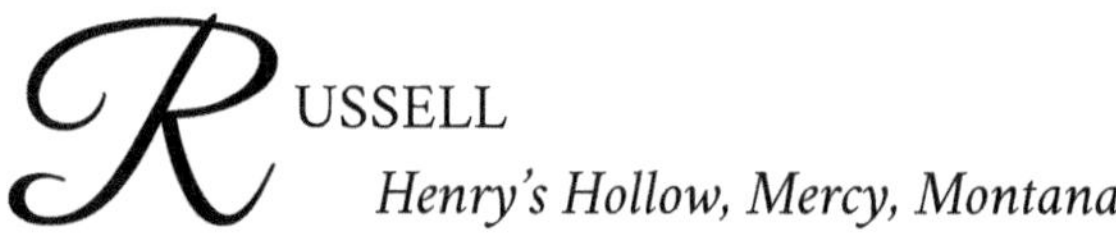

CHAPTER 26

RUSSELL

Henry's Hollow, Mercy, Montana

RUSSELL WATCHED with interest and something he suspected might be close to regret, as the boy's life drained from his eyes. Even though he knew he was defeated, Ethan tried to fight him, his body thrashing under Russell as he applied just enough pressure to his throat to make it last longer than necessary.

He could have shot him, of course, but he'd come to a firm decision that it was an option to be saved as a last resort from then on. It was such a…sterile way of going about something that was so very, very personal.

"What are you thinking right now?" Russell whispered close to Ethan's ear. "Regret? Sadness? Possibly wishing you could cry out for your dear father?" That prompted a fresh burst of resistance, and Russell snickered as the boy flailed weakly and managed to strike him against the side of the head. "Uh-uh," he tsked, pressing harder and adding some extra weight onto

Ethan's chest by lowering himself against him. "I'm afraid your future is already decided."

A flash of pure hatred spread across the boy's face. His nostrils flared and he wheezed as his throat was slowly crushed. Russell was struck again by the similarity between Ethan and his younger brother. The expression of understanding as Daniel had flown down the stairs—

Shaking his head, Russell realized he was sitting up, allowing Ethan to breathe again. Irritated with his lapse in concentration, he moved swiftly and hauled the teen to his feet, putting him in a more traditional headlock. He was allowing himself to become distracted again when he had bigger, more important things to do.

Ethan continued to put up an impressive fight and Russell grunted with the effort it took to keep his arm in place. Because of the commotion, he didn't hear the other noise right away. By the time he looked up, Russell immediately noticed two things: the girl's body was gone, and there was a large dog running at them.

The menacing growl and bared teeth were enough to rattle him more than any other potential threat. Russell dropped Ethan automatically as he went for the gun he'd shoved into his waistband. His breath coming in rapid bursts, Russell stumbled backwards and frantically aimed as the beast bore down on him.

A shot echoed through the cave.

The dog twisted sideways and skid to a stop, cowering in reaction to the sound. Disoriented, she whimpered and altered her course to where Ethan was sitting. Russell frowned at the gun falling from his numb hand as he convulsed, realizing he hadn't fired it. Beyond the boy and dog, Chloe stood in the opening of the cave. A rifle was clasped in her hands, ready to fire again.

"Ugh," Russell mumbled, stepping sideways. His limbs

suddenly went weak and he looked down in confusion at a spreading stain on his shirt. Dropping to his knees, he chuckled, blood frothing on his lips. "I didn't see that coming."

He fell over onto his back and lay staring up at the light seeping in through the natural chimneys. There was a strobing effect undulating through it; lightning from the approaching storm. Or maybe it had already arrived, raging around the cave while their own tempest played out inside.

Russell got lost in the movement of lights and shadows and didn't know how much time had passed before Ethan came to stand over him. Chloe was close behind, holding the weapon as if he were still a threat. Her tan shirt was marred with a patch of dark wetness, but she appeared alert and focused. The dog growled somewhere beyond his vision and Russell could hear her pacing, clearly agitated. Ethan turned and said something inaudible to Chloe before kneeling down next to his side with a look of disgust on his face.

"Who are you?" Ethan asked with genuine curiosity. His eyes narrowed and he wiped at the blood running from his nose before gingerly touching his reddened neck. "Why are you in Mercy?"

"I am no one," Russell gasped. The effort to talk made him cough and warm blood splattered onto the ground by his mouth. "I am everyone. I'm the storm that's come to wash you all away, and you can never stop me. You can't stop something that is already in motion."

"He's insane," Chloe said, her voice sounding far away.

The face above him blurred and Russell strained to focus. "Daniel?" No. No, it was Ethan. And he was dying.

Russell wasn't surprised by his own death. He should have known it would be the boy who would be there to deliver him to it. It all made sense then; his unusual fascination and draw to Ethan. The real reason he'd been led to Mercy. At last, he had found someone who was worthy of living. Russell struggled to reach a hand toward him but his body would no longer respond.

"You failed," Ethan hissed. "You won't hurt anyone else, you sick bastard."

Russell gurgled in response and when he tried again, succeeded in grasping Ethan's hand. Pulling weakly at the boy, the edges of his vision faded, transporting him back to his attic. Russell was lying on his small, lumpy bed, breathing in the stagnant air and staring up at the rough, exposed wooden beams. He hadn't yet taken a life and was ignorant of his greater purpose, though he'd always known there was something different about him. Something special.

Faintly humming the tune of "Edelweiss", his lips damp with blood, Russell left the world smiling.

CHAPTER 27

ENERAL MONTGOMERY
South Gate, Mercy, Montana

As General Montgomery stood staring down the barrel of Sergeant Campbell's weapon, he knew he'd made the critical error of underestimating the man.

The forced self-reflection made him briefly consider the possibility that it was his own vanity that prevented him from predicting the sergeant's treason. Montgomery knew, tactically, that he was right. He had a clear vision of what had to be done in order to preserve the greatest number of lives. His orders should have been followed without question, except that in the current state of things, he was unable to maintain the required control. It allowed for insurrection and uprisings more commonly found in third-world countries.

Mercy was an anomaly. One he planned to capitalize on, especially since it appeared to be in close proximity to the seed vault. Finding Colonel Campbell there with his son and the senator wasn't a complete shock, but was still unexpected and only helped to confirm his suspicions.

The leader of the 1st Force Recon knew Montgomery couldn't afford to let Colonel Campbell get killed. The general didn't like to play games, especially not with his own soldiers. It was time to end the farce and simply acquire what he wanted in another, less direct way on his own terms.

"We all want the same thing," Tom said, holding his hands out in a placating gesture.

"No," Montgomery retorted, his words sharp. "I don't think we do." Turning away from the farmer, he raised a hand to call off his dogs and discovered that while they'd been talking, another group of riders had come up behind them. They were led by a gray-haired man dressed in leather and a worn cowboy hat.

"Jesper Duke," Corporal Dillinger muttered when he spotted him.

"I promised you, Dillinger, that our paths would cross again. You and I have some unfinished business." The old rancher tipped his hat in Tom's direction. "I heard you folks might need a hand."

General Montgomery thrust his arm out in front of Dillinger before he had a chance to answer. The fool had already done enough damage. It was time for him to take control before things got out of hand. He turned to the leader of the SEAL team, who was still squared off with James. "Sergeant—"

"Enough!" Colonel Walsh yelled, startling Montgomery into silence. Moving up next to the general, he held his arms up in surrender. "Stand your men down," he said first to the SEAL leader. "Please," he continued, turning to face James. His head swiveled from Jesper Duke to Tom, the senator, and then back to Montgomery. "It's over, General. I...*we* can't let this go any further."

A clap of thunder rumbled overhead as if on cue and Montgomery could see his soldiers flinch and then look at each other with uncertainty. He didn't care what they thought at the moment. He was concentrating on Walsh and his choice of words.

"I was hoping Mercy wouldn't be so…volatile," Walsh stammered. "And that we could just sort this out later today in a less dramatic fashion. Considering who's involved, I should have known better."

Eyes narrowed, Montgomery took a measured step, closing the gap between them. "Would you care to explain who you mean by 'we'?"

Lowering his arms, Walsh cleared his throat and instead of answering the question, looked over Montgomery's shoulder toward Tom and his group. "Your message got through, Senator. There was a quorum this morning and by now, you should officially be the new president pro tempore."

Betrayal. General Montgomery's face burned with it. The greatest mistake a leader could make was to let their personal feelings cloud their judgement. It was his own fault for allowing the weasel to slide along for far too long. Walsh had been working with Senator Jenson the whole time, undermining him and orchestrating a coup.

His face a mask of anger, the general had a hard time maintaining control of his emotions as he stared at the man whom he thought was a friend. "Arrest him."

When no one moved immediately, he spun toward the SEAL leader and pointed at Walsh. "Arrest the colonel now for treason, or else you'll be next!"

"No!" Walsh yelled back, standing his ground. "General Montgomery, I hereby relieve you of your command by orders of the Joint Commanders, Major General Visor and Sergeant Major O'Shane. You are being charged with conspiring in the assassination of Vice Admiral Baker, conspiring to kidnap Senator Jenson, and ordering—"

Montgomery reached out and grabbed Walsh by the front of his uniform and for a moment, could envision wrapping his hands around the man's throat and squeezing until he could never utter another foul word. But as their eyes met, he saw a truth and understood that none of the accusations could be denied. He had perpetrated them all, and would make no attempt to refute it.

Grunting, the general released Walsh and took a step back, never looking away. "Kelly, you of all people understand why those things had to be done. It was the only way. Our society will crumble and wither away unless we harbor and nurture it."

"It's over, General." Walsh's voice was no longer accusatory but resigned.

"I did it for them," Montgomery urged, gesturing to the people surrounding them in the road. "The soldiers, farmers, and townspeople. The survivors."

"No," Walsh said, shaking his head and taking another step back, like he was repulsed. "You did it for yourself."

Four-star General Andrew Montgomery had always been a virtuous man. He believed in facing the truths of one's own moral character, even when they were hard to accept. He believed in the rule of law and upholding an oath. He blinked, unable to find a valid argument to counter the accusation. Perhaps it was because there was no justification for what he'd been forced to do, but then, he knew that from the first moment he realized he was involuntarily in charge of what was left of the world. He was handed an impossible task; one above the ability of any one man.

Reaching up, Andrew removed the insignia pins from first one shoulder tab, and then the other. Placing the stars in Kelly's hand, he moved past him and made his way past his silent troops and a rancher seeking revenge. Dirt crunched under his polished shoes as he skirted the motionless helicopter and walked down the mountain road, the storm swirling overhead.

Andrew's only regret was that he'd left the old, faded photo of his wife and son in the bottom drawer of a desk, deep inside a mountain he would never return to.

CHAPTER 28

Tom

South Gate, Mercy, Montana

"Let him go." Senator Jenson's order surprised Tom and he looked at her questioningly.

"She's right," Bishop agreed. "It's easier this way."

"How is it easier?" Danny asked, eying the conflicted soldiers nervously. Tom saw that most of them had lowered their weapons and were trying to decide who to take orders from, but a few still had them trained on James and his team.

"It's going to take some time before I'm officially recognized as acting president as well as a lot of work to establish a proper chain of command," Jenson answered while motioning for Walsh to join them. "If Montgomery wants to voluntarily walk away from his post rather than go through a convoluted process, I'm fine with that. The amount of time we'd waste trying to decipher and argue the laws and how they apply in our situation would overshadow what's really important. Even now, we're going to need to rely on a mutual effort between myself and the Joint Commanders. Are you able to act on their behalf?" she asked Walsh.

Colonel Walsh removed a folded piece of paper from his back pocket. "I managed to get a signed declaration from them both before we left, though having you appointed as the acting president will help speed things along."

Tom figured whatever document the soldier named Walsh had was a good thing, based on the senator's reaction. It was clear he'd been working with the civilian government to stop his commander. However, the only thing Tom cared about at the moment was the stand-off that had yet to be resolved. He was acutely aware of how vulnerable they all were, and that his mother and Danny were standing next to him.

He decided to make the first overt move and lowered his rifle the rest of the way. "Why don't we allow the residents of Mercy to return to town while you all figure out who's in charge?" he said loud enough for everyone gathered to hear.

"We have no way of knowing if anything they're saying is true," the SEAL nearest to James barked as the two of them continued to square off. Tom couldn't even guess how a fight between the two would play out, and he didn't want to find out.

"The man standing beside me is Colonel Campbell of the US Army, *Master Chief*," James said evenly, without looking away.

"Again," the Master Chief said with growing agitation. "I have no way of confirming who this guy dressed like a farmer is and last I heard, Sergeant, you were AWOL."

"Stand down, Chief," Walsh directed. When the SEAL leader hesitated, the much smaller man stood rigid and pointed a finger at him. "In case you need a lesson, Chief, I outrank all of you and am now effectively in command of this unit. Are we going to have a problem? Because you're welcome to join Montgomery.

I've heard this part of the state is really quite beautiful, so you might enjoy the hike."

Tom hadn't been sure of his first impression of the colonel, but as he watched the SEAL leader lower his weapon and nod at his men to do the same, he decided he liked the man.

"There's been enough fighting," Walsh continued, stuffing the paper back in his pocket. "From now on, we'll be focusing on rebuilding together, alongside the civilians, and will only invoke our rights under martial law to maintain lawful order for safety."

Several of the soldiers behind Walsh nodded in agreement and looked relieved. Tom imagined most of them weren't that different from the people of Mercy and were only following orders. One of Montgomery's mistakes was that he allowed Dillinger to run with his own agenda and turned a blind eye to what he was doing because it was helping to advance his goals.

Tom knew that kind of mentality was something they'd have to keep dealing with, moving forward. Communication was limited, and with everyone being so isolated, it was easy to make excuses to justify what you had to do in order to survive. The real job of their leaders would be to clearly establish and then maintain the law and order Walsh mentioned. Because it was different now. The world was different and the survivors left behind would have to redefine the rules to fit the new reality.

Turning to the crowd of people behind them, Tom lifted the rifle over his head. "Mercy is safe today!" he shouted, to the cheers and applause of more than three dozen men and women of all ages. "Go back and finish celebrating with your friends and family!"

As the group dispersed, he saw Patty jogging up the road toward him. She was holding the radio and didn't look happy. "Tom!" she yelled, weaving her way through the throng of people.

He winced and grabbed for his own radio before she could reach him. He should have already given an update. "The situation at the south gate is resolved," he said, keying it up. "I repeat, there is no threat. North gate, advise the sergeant that a Colonel Walsh has ordered the military to stand down."

Patty's frown changed to a smile as he finished talking and she waved her radio. "I can do one better than that," she gasped, out of breath from her sprint. "Caleb got on the radio and reached out to the Malmstrom base to see if someone there had enough pull to help us, and he was informed that it's been announced Senator Jenson was voted in as the new president!"

"President Pro Tempore," Senator Jenson corrected. "It means I preside over the senate and am third in line to the succession of the presidency. So, by default, I'll become the acting president. However, I still have to be sworn in and there's a lot to discuss as far as what acting president means, especially in regards to the current martial law and lack of anyone else remaining in the presidential office positions. There's a lot of work to be done," she continued, looking at Walsh. "Which is why I need to get back to Idaho, and then both of us will go to Cheyenne Mountain together."

Colonel Walsh smiled for the first time and gestured to the helicopter. "I think I can help with that, but we still have some unfinished business here."

Tom continued to be impressed by the colonel as he approached him and stuck out a hand. "We haven't been formally introduced, Mr. Miller, though we both know how important it's going to be for us to set the right example for the rest of the country, and potentially what's left of the world."

Shaking Walsh's hand, Tom was struck by the enormity of his words. Somehow, their small town of Mercy had become a central piece to a very complicated puzzle. In that moment, he vowed to do all he could to preserve their way of life, while hosting whatever farming program they came up with to help feed the survivors in the rest of the remaining civilization. It would start there, and hopefully spread until it included everyone.

"We'll do our best," Tom assured him, and then glanced over the colonel's shoulder at Dillinger. The corporal looked like he had a permanent scowl on his face as he glared at Tom, reminding him of what he'd threatened to do. "But I can tell you right now that it isn't going to happen with that man in charge of anything," he added, pointing at Dillinger. "He threatened to slaughter my family in the street just before you arrived, and I believe he would've done it."

"He's already done it!" Jesper Duke yelled, jumping down from his horse. His men mumbled behind him in confirmation and Tom was astounded at the change in Jesper. He'd lost enough weight to look sallow and pale, and his clothes were muddy and torn. Tom guessed it was the result of being chased off his farm and left to scavenge in the woods.

"I was under direct orders and this man resisted," Dillinger said somewhat dismissively. "He made the choice not to comply."

"Choice?" Jesper bellowed. "You shot my son in the *back* as he was running from your men, who were ransacking our property!"

"It's true!" A female soldier dropped down from her horse and approached Walsh and Dillinger. "I was there. The man wasn't a threat and was trying to leave. Corporal Dillinger didn't have to shoot him, and he's done it before."

"Enough!" Dillinger yelled as he turned toward the woman, and Tom reacted automatically when he saw the corporal start to raise his hand as if to strike her.

Lunging forward, Tom grabbed Dillinger's arm, stopping it mid-air. Dillinger spun on him, his other fist coming around, but Tom anticipated it and delivered a solid uppercut before he connected.

The corporal's head snapped up and he staggered back a step, thrown off balance by the unexpected blow. Before he could recover, Sheriff Waters and Bishop each grabbed an arm, while Tom felt Danny pulling him back.

"It's done, Tom," she whispered, wrapping her arms around him from behind and pressing her head against his shoulder.

If it had been anyone else, Tom might have tried to shake them off, but it was Danny. She somehow already knew him better than anyone, and her touch was the one thing that could penetrate his temper. Relaxing, he took a steadying breath and then reached up to squeeze her hands to let her know he was in control.

Releasing him, she moved to his side and then grinned at him as the sheriff manipulated Dillinger's hands into cuffs. "Karma," she whispered.

"Do you have the ability to handle this man back at the mountain?" Senator Jenson asked Walsh.

The colonel rubbed at his jaw while frowning at Dillinger. "I saw enough at the Duke Ranch and Pony Express station to add my own testimony. I know what your orders were, Corporal, and you extended your authority and actions far beyond them. We'll take him back and organize a court martial," he said to the senator.

"I was acting under the direct orders of General Montgomery!" Dillinger spat blood from his mouth, still struggling against the sheriff.

"And you'll have the opportunity to explain that," Walsh replied flatly. "Take him to the helicopter," he directed to the SEAL leader.

The master chief glanced momentarily between his former commander and Walsh and then gave a curt nod. "Yes, sir."

Tom breathed a sigh of relief as he watched the SEAL team escort Dillinger away and he could feel the rest of the tension leave with him. "Jesper," Tom called, motioning to his friend.

"You and your men are welcome in Mercy. We're having a cookout in the center of town and there's plenty for everyone. For all of you," he added, turning back to Walsh.

"We appreciate that," Walsh answered. "But we really need to get the senator to Idaho as quickly as possible, before there's a chance for any unrest. Who's the ranking officer?" he asked the remaining troops.

The woman who had stood up against Dillinger raised her hand. "I am, sir. Lance Corporal Meyers."

"Corporal Meyers, you're to return to Command Center Two and turn all of the land and property back over to the owners. I'll leave it up to you for now to see if you can manage to work together with the farmers in a way that's beneficial to everyone."

"I can help with that," Jesper Duke said, his voice rough. "I don't want to see anyone else hurt during this process. We'll do whatever needs to be done. I appreciate the offer of hospitality," Jesper added, tipping his hat at Tom. "Except the day is still early, and if Corporal Meyers wouldn't mind heading out now, I'd appreciate returning to my family and righting things as soon as possible."

"Sir," Meyers saluted Walsh before doing an about-face and motioning to her unit. "Let's go!"

"We'll arrange a meeting soon," Tom assured Jesper as he pulled his horse about. "We have a lot to talk about."

As Jesper's men and the soldiers began to form an unlikely brigade, Walsh focused again on their need to get moving. "Senator?" he gestured to the helicopter that was already starting to spin up, apparently at the master chief's request.

Senator Jenson nodded but then hesitated, looking at Tom. "I'm going to need an ambassador. Someone to act as a liaison between Mercy and whatever government we establish."

Tom was shaking out his fist, and the pain in his hand made it evident to him that he wasn't the right person for more than one reason. His gaze shifted to his mother, who'd been standing calm and strong next to the senator throughout everything. "I can't think of anyone who'd represent Mercy in that capacity better than my mother."

Sandy raised a hand to her chest and began to shake her head, but Senator Jenson took a hold of her arm and stopped her. "He's right," she said emphatically. "I know enough from our long conversations that you have both the political intelligence needed, as well as the obvious farming experience. Plus, I wouldn't mind getting together over a bottle of wine every once in a while."

Sandy smiled then and the two women hugged. "You might be able to sway me, Senator. Are you sure you have to leave immediately?"

"Timing is critical right now," the senator said, pulling away and looking at each of them before walking over to gaze up at James. "Sergeant, I feel like I have you to thank for this outcome. I know you have some unfinished business and the rest of your family is in California, but when you're settled, we should talk about a special assignment. I have a feeling your dad is going to be in need of a good security team."

James laughed, squinting down at her. "I think you might be right, Senator. And I wonder if you could arrange for some fuel to find its way to my grounded bird?"

Senator Jenson looked back at Walsh, and he scratched at his forehead. "We'll contact Malmstrom. Shouldn't take more than a few days if it's close by."

"Good. We'll make it happen," Jenson assured James. "Not only will you need it to get home to your family, but it'll come in handy for that stretch of road between here and The Farm. Speaking of which," she said while waving a hand at Walsh. "We'll need to make a pit stop. I lost my head of security along the way." Walsh stared at her and tilted his head questioningly.

"It's a long story. I'll tell ya on the way. I'm just glad we don't have to walk."

Tom stood silently as everyone said their final goodbyes. He had mixed emotions about the senator leaving and the unstable political atmosphere she was about to attempt to control. So long as Mercy didn't end up in the middle of a power struggle, the role they played was theirs to define. Senator Jenson seemed like a woman of her word, and with his mom helping bridge any gaps, he felt more secure about Mercy's future.

Once the wind from the helicopter died down and the aircraft was heading toward the distant mountains, there was nothing left to do but go back and finish their celebration. As Danny reached for his hand, another bolt of lightning cut through the churning clouds overhead and momentarily turned the sky abnormally orange. It was a good reminder that the military might prove to be the easiest hurdle to get over.

"Let's get back," Danny urged, cringing from the ensuing thunder. "And we should make sure the soldiers at the north gate believed us. Hopefully they have a way of contacting their base to confirm everything."

"Caleb can help with that if it's an issue," Patty suggested.

Tom had so many different thoughts tumbling through his head that he'd forgotten again about the other group of soldiers. Picking up his pace, he gave Danny's hand a tug. "Whose idea was it that I become mayor?" he said with a crooked grin.

"I hate to jump right back into politics," Bishop interrupted as he kept pace with them. "But things are going to move fast. I'd suggest another meeting with the town leaders so we can fill them in on everything, including The Farm. We'll be called upon soon to make some big decisions as a town."

"We?" Danny asked, still smiling.

Bishop looked over to where James was walking with his men, and then at Sandy. "I hope I'm not being presumptuous, but

I'll need to stay close in order to oversee The Farm. I suppose I could operate out of the office, but if you'll have me, I'd rather assign Hicks there and remain a part of Mercy."

Sandy moved around Tom and hooked her arm through Bishop's. "I wouldn't have it any other way. The Miller Farm wouldn't be the same without you."

Bishop began to smile, but then glanced at Tom expectantly. Tom appreciated the show of respect, though it wasn't necessary. Stopping, he extended a hand to the older man. "We'd be happy to have you. Just don't ever do anything that'll result in me getting my butt handed to me again."

When Sandy rose her eyebrows at him, Tom shook his head. "Another time, Mom." She was about to insist on more details, when the sound of a running horse drew Tom's attention and he was surprised to see Tango come charging around a bend in the road.

"Dad!" Ethen yelled. "I'm glad we found you. What's going on? We saw the helicopter leaving."

As Tango got closer, Grace trailed behind them, and it was obvious Ethan had been pushing the horse. Tom frowned when he saw the blood on Ethan's face and a fresh shiner forming on at least one of his eyes. When Chloe peeked out from behind Ethan, Tom already knew something was very wrong.

"You're bleeding!" Sandy cried as Tango stopped near them.

"What in the world happened to you two?" Tom demanded, immediately on guard when he saw there was also blood on Chloe's shirt. "Are there more soldiers up at the spring?"

"What? No!" Ethan retorted, wiping warily at his face. "What soldiers?"

"I'm fine," Chloe gasped, holding tightly to Ethan. She looked dazed as Bishop ran to help her.

"The military showed up, and we managed to work it out,"

Sheriff Waters intervened while gesturing to Ethan. "Right now, I think you might have a more urgent matter to fill us in on."

"She was shot," Ethan said without preamble. "By Father Rogers."

"I wasn't shot!" Chloe argued, wincing as Bishop lifted her down. "It's just a graze."

Tom had moved to take Tango's reins and froze at his son's words, his breath catching.

"Wait." Patty looked pale. "What do you mean? Father Rogers did this? Where? Why?"

Danny knelt down as Grace leaned into her and she ran a hand down the dog's back. "There's blood on her!" she exclaimed.

"It's mostly mine," Ethan said, still on Tango. He met Tom's fierce gaze with an intensity a boy his age shouldn't possess. "Grace saved our lives, Dad. And you know how you told me to stay out of Henry's Hollow?"

Tom blinked. "Henry's Hollow?" He was having a hard time following what his son was saying. None of it made any sense. "Was there a cave-in?"

"No," Ethan said quickly. "It was almost something a whole lot worse."

"We'll all need to sit down for this one," Chloe said grimly. "But let's just say nothing good *ever* happens in a cave."

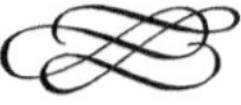

CHAPTER 29

S TEVIE
Northwestern Washington State

STEVIE DREW a thick line across another day on the calendar with a Sharpie and took a deep, shuddering breath. He normally marked the days off in the morning, but he'd forgotten until the sun was going down and he noticed it wasn't done yet. He was doing that a lot lately. Forgetting things.

Twenty-four days since "it" happened. That was more than three weeks. Dropping the calendar back onto the kitchen table, it knocked an empty can of pop off and Stevie watched it clatter across the floor. At first, he'd been very careful about picking trash up because he knew if he made a mess his mom would have a conniption when she got home. That was part of the deal they made at the beginning of summer. If he got to stay home while she worked, he would have to clean up after himself.

Snoopy whined and nudged his hand that was hanging limply down by the side of the chair. Stevie gave up early on trying to get the dog to answer to Slayer, so Snoopy it was. "What?" he muttered, turning his hand over so the lab could lick it. "I'm okay, buddy. Just tired, is all."

They were running out of food, and had been for a few days. Stevie scavenged as much as he could from the vacant houses near him. He still had several cans of vegetables and corn, but he didn't think it was giving him enough of what his body needed, since all of the good stuff was gone. Good food like chili, peanut butter, candy bars, and chips. Well…he knew the chips didn't have much in them, but the other stuff at least had fat and calories and made his brain feel better.

Stevie kinda felt like the time when he got the flu and had to stay home in bed for a week. His body hurt, and it was hard to think. He supposed he wasn't starving yet, except he might if something didn't change.

He'd gotten the barbeque to work the second week, and began boiling water to drink. He even caught a few fish. Then, the rains started and the fish stopped biting. The grass was turning brown, even though it rained a ton. Stevie thought there might be something wrong with the rain, though it didn't do anything bad to him.

Kicking at the soda can, he was suddenly very angry. Nothing was right, and he didn't know what to do anymore. Stevie looked at the back door and his backpack that was stuffed with supplies, ready to go. If he ever made up his mind to leave.

The propane feeding the barbeque would run out soon, so he'd need to start making regular fires to boil water or cook. He's only found one lighter and that wouldn't last forever. He could go look through the house's junk drawers for more, but Stevie was just so…tired. Of scavenging, of being dirty, of not knowing what was happening, or if his mom was alive.

His breath caught and Stevie wiped roughly at his nose. He

told himself he wouldn't cry like a baby anymore about his mom. It'd been a *month*. He'd been alone for almost a month.

"She isn't coming back, Snoopy," he yelled at the dog, as if it was his fault. Snoopy only looked at him with his brown, sad eyes and whined again. Feeling instantly guilty, Stevie dropped from the chair and onto his knees so he could grasp Snoopy's face in his hands and rest his forehead against the dog's. "I'm sorry. You're a good boy. You're a good boy, Snoopy." Snoopy thumped his tail happily and licked at Stevie's face, forgiving him of all his sins.

Stevie wasn't sure he deserved it. He didn't think he was being a good provider for his best friend. He didn't know how to hunt, other than fishing, and he was afraid to go farther than the ten houses he'd already searched. A few days earlier, he'd ventured beyond what he called the "safe zone", and nearly been shot. People were crazy now. They'd kill you for a glass of water, let alone some of the good kind of food. He suspected they would eat Snoopy if he got caught by the wrong people. Maybe even him, too.

Stevie shook his head at the thought, still nose-to-nose with Snoopy. "Uh-uh. We can't go into other houses, Snoop. It's too dangerous. I'm either gonna have to figure out how to go all caveman and make fires and hunt and stuff, or try to go to Jay's."

He remembered how to get to his best friend's house, it was just so *far*. A half-hour in a car, so probably around two hours on his bike, was Stevie's best guess. Last summer, he tried to ride his bike there after his mom told him he couldn't spend the night. He made it halfway before she tracked him down and grounded him for a month.

It wasn't that Stevie didn't think he could go that far, it was the people in between that scared him. That they might try to steal his bike, or his bag, or his dog. He saw a group with horses two days ago, only two blocks away and inside the "safe zone".

They were long, country blocks, but it was close enough that seeing them made him feel sick. Like, he nearly puked on his shoes while hiding behind some bushes.

The men were dirty, and some of them were bloody. They had guns and after they went into one of the houses Stevie had been thinking about visiting, he heard a gunshot. He had no way of knowing if they killed someone or not, but that was sure what it looked like.

That was why, even though he was running out of food, and gonna run out of propane, and he had his bag all packed…he was still sitting in his kitchen. Stevie was afraid so much of the time that his gut had a permanent knot in it. Like all the fear was moving through his body and going straight to his stomach, where it hardened into a ball that was getting bigger and bigger until one day it was just going to explode.

Snoopy's ears pricked up and his gentle whine turned into a low growl.

Stevie jerked upright on the hard, wooden chair and held his breath. Snoopy had much better hearing than him and warned him once when another mean dog was out in the front yard.

There!

The sound of gravel crunching. Crunching?

Stevie jumped to his feet and made his way through the shadowy family room so he could peer out the front window. His breath caught when he saw a horse-drawn cart at the end of their long driveway. There were several people standing next to it and they were dressed like the men he'd seen before. The ones he needed to hide from.

Running back to the kitchen, he grabbed his backpack and took the stairs to the second floor two at a time. In his room, he had a ridiculous thought that he needed to find the box of his favorite action figures to take with him, and he struggled for a few wild heartbeats to control his breathing so he could think more clearly. He was panicking. Stevie knew he was panicking and he was gonna get killed if he didn't stop it and think straight.

The front door banged open. He froze, then forced himself to tip-toe to his bedroom window. It was already open, the screen removed, and he slipped out onto the porch roof that faced the back of the house. He turned to whisper to Snoopy, but the black lab was already leaping out after him. Pulling the curtain back across the opening, he then eased out as far as he dared, and lay flat on his stomach.

He'd come up with the escape plan late the night before. If he was lucky, the scavengers would go through the house and leave without ever knowing he was there. They'd have no reason to look out his bedroom window, unless he gave them one. Throwing an arm over Snoopy, who was lying down next to him, he hummed softly in the dog's ear to calm him and keep him from whining or barking.

"Steven!" A muffled voice yelled from the kitchen below him.

Stevie stopped humming.

"Stevie! Are you here?" The voice was louder as they came up the stairs.

Stevie closed his eyes and swallowed hard. He had to be delusional. He was finally losing it.

There were noises in his room for what felt like forever, then the curtain above his head was drawn back and a woman's face appeared. "Stevie? Oh praise God, is that really you?"

Stevie looked up, and his mouth hanging open as his throat constricted with emotion, preventing him from crying out. Her face was bruised and it looked like she had stitches in her forehead, but he would always recognize his mom. Of course, she would be the one person who would know to look for him out on the roof. It was where they always use to lay together and watch the stars, before the world fell apart.

As the reality washed through him, the fear was chased away

and Stevie's eyes filled with tears of relief. He finally found his voice as the woman crawled through the window and scooped him into her arms, sobbing uncontrollably.

"Mom!" he cried.

She'd come home.

CHAPTER 30

CHLOE

Miller Ranch, Mercy, Montana

THE STORM finally hit with a vengeance late the night before and then stopped abruptly just before dawn. Chloe thought it mirrored their own intense experiences from the Fourth of July. Except unlike the fresh, crisp air the rain left behind, she continued to feel burdened by her run-in with Russell.

Chloe focused on her breathing and stared at her feet as they pounded on the dirt trail. She knew the exercise and familiar routine would help calm her nerves, even though her side ached with each jarring step.

"You were shot in the chest and you're still faster than me!" Ethan gasped from behind, his voice straining with the effort to keep up.

Chloe slowed and grinned at him when he came alongside her. "Quit being so dramatic." They'd gotten an early start and were already headed back to the farm as the sun crested the mountains and began to warm the air. She stopped to give her ribs a break, and soak up the peaceful energy in her favorite grove of evergreens. "Dr. Olsen even said it's only a scrape."

Ethan's face pinched up and he wagged a finger at her. "I believe what she said was that the bullet scraped your rib, which prevented it from going *into* your chest. Pretty sure I saw some bone in that *scrape*."

Chloe rolled her eyes before taking off again, determined to prove that she wasn't really injured. She knew it was silly, but it made her feel better. If she could shrug off nearly getting killed, then it made the rest of the traumatic encounter easier to handle.

"I think you got the worse end of the deal," Chloe said without any humor. She kept her pace slow enough so that Ethan could stay beside her, and she stared at him critically. One eye was almost completely swollen shut and the other had some bruising spreading under it. His neck was scratched and there were so many bands of color across it that he looked like someone had taken a paintbrush to him. Only, it wasn't a painting, and Chloe saw it as a painful reminder of how close they'd both come to dying. The irony of it all was enough to make her scoff whenever she thought about it. After everything, some freak posing as a priest was what almost did them in.

"What do you think he was?" Ethan asked, clearly having similar thoughts to Chloe, and ignoring her observations about his own injuries.

Chloe shrugged. "Your guess is as good as mine. You heard what Bishop said last night. They didn't find any ID in his stuff, except for the deputy badge and nametag. We'll probably never know who he really was."

"No." Ethan reached out and took ahold of her arm, gently pulling her to a stop and forcing her to face him. "That's not what I mean. *What* was he, Chloe?"

A chill she'd been working hard to suppress since the first

time she'd seen the man in Henry's Hollow slithered around her chest, causing a fresh flare of pain in her damaged rib. Absently raising her free hand to press at the wound, Chloe swallowed hard and returned Ethan's intense gaze. Yes, she knew what he meant. "Something I hope we never see again."

Nodding slowly, Ethan glanced around at the thick trees, clearly spooked by the conversation. "We should get back now. Grandma's going to start breakfast early, and Crissy and Trevor should be getting here soon so we can get up to the lake on time."

He was referring to the special meeting Tom had called to fill the town leaders in on the details they'd been missing out on. Trevor and Crissy would be coming with Dr. Olsen. Chloe wouldn't be surprised if Crissy told her she'd decided to live with Melissa. Turned out she was a natural at being a medical assistant, and ever since the attack, Crissy was a nervous wreck while at the ranch.

Chloe thought it was smart to hold the meeting on the farm, and Tom's choice to take them up to a lookout over Mercy was only fitting. They would, after all, be talking about the whole town's future. Which was now also *her* future.

Before Ethan could pull away, Chloe stepped forward and kissed him briefly on the lips. Smiling, he looked at her questioningly. "What was that for?"

"For being you." Chloe didn't know how else to say it. Ethan was the best friend she'd ever had, and the bond they shared was something she knew would last through anything.

It must have been the right thing to say, because his expression became serious as he hugged her tightly before abruptly letting go. Jogging backwards, he waved a hand in the air. "I have a confession. I was holding back this whole time, so if you want any chance of eating some of the leftover steak, you're gonna have to *run!*"

Laughing, Chloe chased after him, feeling so much lighter

than when they'd started. The darkness they faced in the cave was something that rubbed off on them. It couldn't be explained, but they both felt it. Together was the best way to overcome it, and Chloe was sure that with time, it would be a piece of the memory rather than a part of them.

"Chloe!" Bishop shouted from nearby, jarring her from her thoughts and causing her to focus again on where she was.

They'd entered the upper field and Chloe saw Bishop was partway down the trail, on his way to the house. He was holding a stack of notebooks and looking rather serious, even for Bishop.

"I wanted a chance to talk with you before the meeting," he said once she reached him. Lifting the notebooks, he frowned at them. "These are all the transcripts from my radio transmissions, and I stayed up most of the night writing down all the details about The Farm and vault program."

"Okay." Chloe stared at him quizzically, not sure what it was he wanted her to say.

"Chloe, I've betrayed a lot of people's trust and I know I'm going to need to prove myself to them." Bishop hesitated before looking behind them to where James and his team was busy breaking down their camp at the far end of the field. "But I want to make sure we're okay. I want you to know that no matter what happens with The Farm, or even James, I'm not going to stop trying to find your parents. I consider you a part of my family now, and family never abandons each other."

One of the things Chloe appreciated about Bishop was that he was a man whose word meant something. He might not have been forthcoming about who he really was, but anything he'd ever done or said was genuine and Chloe knew she could rely on him. If Bishop said he was going to find her parents, he would. Or, at least find out what happened to them. And he was right; they were family now. Just like Miller Ranch was her home.

"Of course we're okay," she said with a smile. "My only

problem now is that I don't know if I should call you Bishop, Carl, Colonel, or Mr. Campbell."

Laughing, he put an arm around her shoulder and they began to walk together toward the farm. "Bishop. I think I've always preferred that man."

"Me too," Chloe agreed, thinking back over the past month and all that had happened, including her own personal growth. She was different. In some ways, she'd need time to heal and rediscover some aspects of herself and how to get over being forced to take another life. In other ways, she was a better person. Stronger, and kinder, because of the people she'd come to know, including Bishop.

Leaning into Bishop's arm, Chloe had no idea what their future was going to look like, but so long as they were all together, it would be okay. *She* would be okay.

CHAPTER 31

DANNY
Miller Ranch, Mercy, Montana

DANNY WAS CONFLICTED by the contrasting scenery as they rode three abreast on the trail to the lake. Her dad and Sam were talking amiably beside her while she absorbed the early morning sun, birdsong, and aroma of warmed pine needles and wet hay. However, mixed in with the seemingly charming setting was the browning grass and lingering odd cloud formations. The birds pleasantly twittering could take flight into erratic and sometimes suicidal patterns without warning, which always made Danny apprehensive when she heard them.

To someone who hadn't experienced the past twenty-five days, the tranquil countryside would have appeared almost normal, but they all knew the truth. It was going to be a long struggle that would likely involve ongoing changes before any sort of standard measure of normalcy could be set.

"Bishop said James and his unit are getting ready to leave in a couple of hours," Sam was telling Tane. "Apparently, they're based out of Southern California, which is being hammered by storms worse than we're experiencing. They've got to get their families before they can come back and settle into any sort of role here."

"They're going to stop here first after getting refueled though, right?" Danny interrupted, concerned. Bishop assured her the night before that he would get a message through to the Malmstrom base about sending some medication with the soldiers delivering the fuel. In addition to the desperately needed antibiotics and insulin, he'd requested the beta blockers for her dad. Danny wasn't sure the base infirmary would give up the more popular meds, but she was hoping the heart medication wouldn't be in high demand.

"They'll be flying right back over. Mercy is on their way to Idaho," Sam said with a nod. "I'm sure the senator will stop if they've got anything, Danny."

Sam knew how concerned she was about her dad, and that he'd gone without his meds now for a couple of days. He was a good friend, and she appreciated how positive he remained, in spite of his own suffering that he never mentioned, let alone complained about.

Tane cleared his throat and leaned forward enough that he could look over at Danny. "I think I'll be fine without the medicine for a bit. Turns out all these outdoor activities and eating only fresh food has helped me shed quite a few pounds. It's a much healthier lifestyle. I'm feeling better than I have in a long time."

Danny's initial response was to remind her father that no amount of lifestyle change could reverse the damage to his heart, but she bit back the words. He knew that already and certainly didn't need her telling him. Instead, she smiled reassuringly. "You look great, Dad."

Grace suddenly lunged past them and leapt off the trail as they neared the lake, barking happily and running in a wide circle around Lilly, who was tied to a tree. Danny knew Tom was close by and turned her horse from the trail to follow the golden retriever. "I'll meet you up there!" she called to Sam and her father, feeling better than she thought she would as they rode off together. Sam's positive attitude had a way of rubbing off on people, and Danny knew from experience that it absolutely helped when someone had a chronic health issue. She needed to learn from her friend and take each day as it came, instead of worrying so much about the future.

Reaching Lilly, she dropped from her horse and tied the mare up while laughing at Grace's antics. The dog had been to the lake on a number of occasions, yet she still got so excited about the water that she was worse than a small child. Picking up a stick, Danny tossed it out into the body of water to make Grace happy.

She'd been to the lake herself on more than one occasion, so she felt pretty sure of where she'd find Tom. After a quick hike around the far end, Danny located him at what he claimed was his favorite fishing hole. "Any luck?" she called out when she spotted his pole sticking out of the trees.

"Nah." Tom pulled the line from the water and met her partway, holding out a hand to help her over some logs. "I didn't really expect to catch any, not after that storm last night. It was more to clear my head. This place has a good way of doing that."

Danny frowned at him, picking up on the tension in his shoulders and the lines in his forehead. "What's got you so worried?"

"The whole reason Patty stepped down and apparently appointed me as mayor was because of her losing the confidence of the city council," Tom explained, looking out over the placid lake. "One of the first things I did was withhold information from them that nearly got Mercy destroyed. It's going to take some work to gain their trust back and I'm not sure how to do it."

"Tom." Danny said his name tersely and he looked at her with some surprise. "You need to stop apologizing for yourself all the time. Yeah, you've made some mistakes, but we all have. You literally knew about that seed vault for a day, and it wasn't even your secret to tell. If you feel some great need to ask the council and town leaders for forgiveness over this, then go ahead. Personally, I think you should own up to your choices with self-assurance. That's what Patty sees in you, and why the people of Mercy want to follow you. You have the ability to make hard choices when the chips are down and what they all need right now is to see that confidence."

Tom's shoulders relaxed and he grinned at Danny, taking her other hand in his. "See? This is why I need you here on the farm with me. Everything else aside, you give amazing advice."

Danny moved in closer and looked up at Tom, enjoying his nearness and the strength she always drew from him. "Are you asking me to move in with you, Mr. Miller?"

Tom blushed and searched her face, trying to tell if she was serious. "Well, I've been hoping you might decide to stay."

"Only if you're willing to share me with Chief Martinez," she said innocently, batting her eyes at him.

Frowning, Tom opened his mouth to ask a question and then closed it again, struggling for the right words. Laughing, Danny put a hand on this chest and gave him a reassuring kiss. "Don't worry, Mayor. I'll let you court me properly, and I was referring to my taking three shifts a week at the fire station. Chief Martinez has his own farm that's been suffering for the past month, so I thought I could help out and also work at the clinic on those days."

Shaking his head at her, Tom smiled good-naturedly. "I think it's a great idea. I'll be riding into town most days to take care of my mayoral duties, as Patty likes to call it, so we can check in with each other."

Danny followed Tom out of the cove after he retrieved his pole and they headed back to the horses. Grace found them, still grasping the wet stick in her mouth, so Danny threw it again to the dog's utter delight. "Be careful what you wish for," she said with a more casual tone. "You might end up getting tired of being around me so much."

Turning to her near Lilly, Tom surprised Danny by reaching out and cupping her face with both of his hands. She noticed how careful he was not to bump the small dressing on her ear, and it made her love him even more.

"One of the few things in this life I'm still sure of is the fact that I'll never get tired of being with you," Tom said with such sincerity that Danny was speechless. He kissed her gently then before letting her go. "Don't ever forget that."

She wouldn't. Standing there in a place she would have never dreamt of being only a month before, Danny had somehow miraculously found love. She wished it hadn't taken the end of the world for her to face her demons, but through the inconceivable experiences, she finally knew who she was again. A strong, independent woman with broad shoulders, and an even bigger heart.

CHAPTER 32

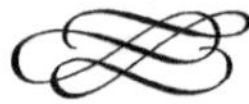

ETHAN
Miller Farm, Mercy, Montana

BY THE TIME Ethan and Chloe reached the lookout, council members were starting to arrive and his dad was already there, leaning on a fence from a safe distance. He knew his dad was probably running over what he was going to say, but Ethan needed a minute with him.

"Find us a seat?" he said, turning to Chloe.

Chloe grinned in response, since they'd be standing in an open grassy area. "Go," she said, shooing him away, understanding the real request.

Ethan glanced out over the open expanse as he neared his dad. He was always awestruck by the view up there, no matter how many times he saw it. The particular ledge they were perched on was high up on the west side of the valley with a sweeping vista in every other direction, including the town of Mercy. In spite of the unusual colors streaked through the clouds as the sun continued to rise, and the browning foliage that was becoming more apparent every day, it still made Ethan feel safe. It was their valley, their home, and they would continue to protect it. He knew his dad would do whatever was necessary, and that also gave him courage.

"Hey, Dad," he called out.

Tom looked pleased to see him, instead of being annoyed at having his solitude interrupted. "I'm glad you came over," he said, lifting a hand up toward Ethan. "I've been waiting for you. I wanted to give you this."

Confused, Ethan stared at the dull-colored rock in the palm of his dad's hand. It took him a moment. When he finally recognized it as the trilobite Ed Hanson gave him on the second day after the flashpoint, unexpected tears sprang to his eyes. "You've had it this whole time? I thought I'd lost it, when…you know."

"When Decker and Billy took you," Tom finished for him, his voice rough.

Ethan placed his hand over the fossil and looked up at his dad. He was surprised to see he was fighting to control his emotions, something that didn't happen very often.

"I found it in the road when I woke up," Tom continued after clearing his throat. "I made a vow to myself then that I would find you, Ethan. I knew I would because you're a survivor. I knew you'd never give up and I want this to serve as a reminder to you. No matter what's happened, the things done to you or what you've been forced to do, remember that you're a survivor in life and in staying true to yourself."

Although it was exactly what Ethan needed to hear, he didn't know if he believed any of it. After his encounter with Russell and what the guy had said to him, he'd been having a hard time shaking off the feeling that maybe he was right. With all the darkness Ethan experienced the past month, maybe it wasn't possible to come through it without losing a part of himself.

"How do I even know who I am anymore?" he gasped, looking away from his dad.

"Because I'm your father and I know who you are!" Tom said forcefully, taking ahold of Ethan's shoulders and turning him so he'd have to look at him. "You sacrificed yourself first to save me. Then you risked your life for Danny and Sam, and repeatedly suffered personally in exchange for the safety of Chloe and so many others. That's what a hero is, Ethan. I'm proud of you and the man you've become and I would be honored if you worked with me in the mayor's office. I'm going to need a lot of help coordinating the farming program with our town, The Farm, and the government. Will you help me?"

Ethan was stunned. He remembered how he'd clung to the need for his father's approval like a lifeline when everything first started falling apart. He couldn't remember when, but at some point, it stopped mattering as much. Now that he had his father's respect, it meant more than he could have ever imagined.

Standing up a little straighter, Ethan clasped his fist around the trilobite and reached out toward his father with the other. When his dad gripped his hand, it wasn't the pacifying motion of an adult trying to please a child, but a firm, powerful handshake between two men. "I'd be honored to work with you, Dad."

Clenching his jaw, Ethan gave his father a brisk nod before turning away, not trusting himself to say anything further. Walking back to where Chloe waited for him, he glanced over at Tango and then to his grandmother, who was coming up the path.

Ethan understood then how he already had everything he needed to define himself, and clutching the trilobite close to his chest, decided he liked what he saw.

CHAPTER 33

Tom

Miller Ranch, Mercy, Montana

As Ethan walked away, Tom's chest swelled with pride. He knew exactly what sort of inner turmoil Ethan was dealing with, because he was struggling with the same emotions. In many ways, his son had gone through more than he had, and held up better under the pressure. Tom meant what he said; he was proud of Ethan and the man he'd become.

After hearing the story the night before about the confrontation with Russell Rogers, if that was even his real name, Tom was disturbed that he'd failed to recognize the danger lurking among them. It was a threat none of them had expected, or were prepared for. It was the sort of evil he suspected would rise up in the ruins of their society and if they weren't careful, cause more destruction than the more obvious sources.

Fear and hate festered like a wound until it spilled over, unless it was treated properly. For Mercy to stay healthy and flourish, Tom knew that full disclosure and working together so that they operated in unity was required. He understood now why Patty was so distressed by the suicide that happened during her watch. That kind of despair was to be expected, of course, but the only way to combat it was by caring enough about each other to notice and intervene.

The clearing was filling up with the council members, town leaders, and his family and friends. He didn't ask them there to give a speech or lecture, but to look out together over their town while he explained Mercy's role in the coming months and years. It was critical that they all agreed to be a part of it. That they *wanted* to be.

"Your dad would be proud."

Tom smiled at his mom as she approached him, reflecting on the similarity of her words and the ones he'd just had with Ethan. "I hope so, Mom. I miss him every day."

Sandy scooted through the space in the railings and then leaned next to him, bumping him playfully in the shoulder. "I know you do. We all miss him, but he's never very far away."

Gazing out at the valley, she tilted her face to the breeze, strands of her dark hair billowing around her face. "You have to give them hope, Tom."

Grace had been gleefully running around to greet everyone, and had finally settled down by Lilly. Laying near the large horse, she rested her head on her paws while gazing up at the other animal. It was such a simple reminder for Tom. How Grace had trusted him during the fire when she was most vulnerable and struggling to breathe. She'd allowed him to drape her across the back of a horse and carry her to safety.

Tom knew what his mom meant. In the middle of all the chaos and hopelessness, they had to find and hold on to the moments that made them feel. The way saving Grace that one afternoon had broken through his turmoil and made him reconnect with a part of himself he had almost lost. Those emotions were what compelled them to do the right thing. It gave them hope.

Tom never thought he'd be more than a father and a rancher, and he'd had those roles, as well as several others, challenged over the past month. He wasn't always proud of how he'd reacted, and in some ways, he'd failed, but Danny was right. It was okay to own up to the failures, and even more important to embrace his success.

Taking his mother's hand in his, Tom reminded himself that one of those roles was as a son. "Come on," he said, giving her a tug. "Let's go talk to our friends together."

As Tom and Sandy walked down the trail and toward the people representing their town, he drew strength from the love he felt for each of them, and the energy of the land itself. Danny, Ethan, Sam, Bishop, Chloe, and James. They had all been called home for different reasons and were now part of something much bigger than their own needs. Through a complex web of circumstances, they were now in a position to give hope not just to their own community, but the rest of the country.

Stopping near the top of the lookout, surrounded by the wooded mountains and raw beauty of the land, Tom finally allowed himself to acknowledge that he'd made it. They were home. A sob worked its way through his body to escape as a moan that was part despair over what had been lost, and part relief for what was gained. He didn't try to hide it as others saw his powerful emotions released. It was okay to feel, to love, and to hold on to whatever gave you joy. Through it all, they had found each other.

Together, they found Mercy.

THE END